The Ugly Girlfriend

The Lonely Heart Series

Latrivia S. Nelson

RIVERHOUSE
PUBLISHING

The Ugly Girlfriend
RiverHouse Publishing, LLC
5100 Poplar Avenue
Suite 2700
Memphis, TN 38117

All **RiverHouse, LLC** Titles, Imprints and Distributed Lines are available at special quantity discounts for bulk purchases for sales promotions, premiums, fund-raising and educational or institutional use.

First RiverHouse, LLC Trade Paperback Printing: 08/01/2011

1

ISBN: 978-0-9832186-4-7
ISBN: 0-9832-1864-7

Printed in the United States of America

This book is printed on acid-free paper.

www.riverhousepublishingllc.com

This book is dedicated to my faithful fans, blog participants and radio show listeners. There is beauty in all of us, but we must know that fact before anyone else can see it. I hope that you enjoy.

Helena:

"Love looks not with the eyes but with the mind."

A Midsummer Night's Dream (I, i, 234)

William Shakespeare

Acknowledgments

Karen Moss, thanks for taking time to help me clean up my messy manuscripts. You are a valued reader, and I truly appreciate you. Thanks for being my angel and having so much patience.

Thanks to the team at RiverHouse Publishing including Kandace, Megan, Crystal and Jack.

Thanks to my family for being patient with me.

Thanks to every fan. I have received, printed and read each email, letter, text, Facebook message, Twitter message, etc. Each means so much to me. I'm so happy to have you as readers, and I'm grateful for your friendships.

Chapter One

Club Play Pen was packed nearly past code violation with yuppies and athletes by midnight. Blaring house music and multi-colored strobe lights added chaos to the crowds intermingling between the inside of the club and the open patio leading out to the cool breeze of downtown Phoenix.

While everyone else seemingly enjoyed themselves, LaToya Jenkins rounded the dance floor with her frozen drink carefully tucked into the tight embrace of her hands, avoiding the small hovels of *prim* and *proper* women to get to the booth where her friends waited for her.

This wasn't exactly her scene. It was her close friend, Angela, 35th birthday, and in celebration, the girls had agreed to take her out. So, here LaToya was in a crowded club being ignored by the entire male population *again*, while Angela gyrated on the dance floor with the tenth guy on her dance card.

"Sorry it took so long," LaToya apologized with a huff as she arrived back at the booth. Her two friends looked up from their conversation and scooted over in unison to give her some room.

LaToya was a big girl. Well, she was bigger than they were. Gracefully toting a few extra pounds, she was the heaviest of her little clique of four. Size 14 to be exact and *heavy chested*, as her mother had called her.

She pushed into the leather booth and sat her drink in front of her. The prickles of her pantyhose rubbed against her legs and clung to her sweaty thighs.

I hate these things, she thought to herself as she tried to put on a happy face. Inside, she wished that she could have been at home curled up to a good book.

"What took you so long, girl?" Deana asked, moving her long, black weave from her oval face with her French-tipped acrylic nail.

"The bartender kept ignoring me," LaToya answered frustrated. "*But* I finally got a guy to order for me." The young, female bartender scantily dressed in a purple *peek-a-boo* outfit straight out of *Fredrick's of Hollywood* had ignored anyone who wasn't extremely handsome or a size zero, which was why she had finally resorted to outsourcing her order to someone more desirable.

"A guy, huh?" Kristen, her other friend chimed in. "What did the chivalrous knight look like? Rich? Powerful? Cute?"

"All of the above. He's one of my clients," LaToya explained with a faint grin. "I ran into him outside of the bathroom. So, when he came up to the bar, I asked him to get my drink."

Pulling the straw to her lips, she sipped her drink. *Too strong*, she thought to herself as she pushed it away. *All of that effort for nothing. Figures.*

"You said all of the above?" Kristen continued. "Where is he?"

LaToya turned in the booth and looked towards the bar. From their elevated position over the dance floor, she could clearly see the large man. He was still standing in the same position talking to a group of women and laughing. Once she was sure that he wouldn't notice her, she pointed towards him. "The tall brother in the white shirt," she said, taking another sip of her drink. *She might as well get her money's worth.* "His name is Byron. He's an architect for the biggest firm in Phoenix."

All eyes quickly shifted towards the bar. She could feel their collective attention drawing towards *the money*.

"Where?" Kristen asked squinting. "There are like six men over there with white shirts on."

Deana hastily slid on her glasses and scanned the room.

LaToya was always amazed at her friends and their shameless pursuits of the overrated opposite sex. "He's the really dark brother with the jeans on and the white button down shirt. He's right there by the white guy," she said, pointing again.

"Oh, now I see him." Kristen licked her lips. Her hazel-contact clad eyes widened.

"He sees us too," Deana said, pulling at the sides of her strapless dress.

"Look, look, he's waving," Kristen said in a high pitched voice.

They all waved back, including LaToya, who was simply glad that she knew someone worth knowing in this place.

"Oh snap. He's coming over." Kristen turned quickly. She pulled out her compact and checked her lipstick.

Deana followed suit.

"Why do you two bother? You look amazing," LaToya said to her friends.

"*And* he's bringing over the white boy. So, someone gets the leftovers," Deana giggled as she eyed them from her mirror.

LaToya didn't bother to *freshen up*. She knew that they weren't coming over to talk to her. This was the exact same thing that happened every time that they all went out. The men gathered to talk to her friends and completely ignored her.

Minutes later, Byron strode confidently to their booth with his friend in tow. They smiled like Cheshire cats, eyeing the women who quietly cooed after them.

"Good evening, Ladies," Bryon greeted over the music while looking at LaToya. His bright brown eyes sparkled with mischief. He knew that he was a catch. And so did they.

Byron was the normal *Ebony Man of the Year*. Tall. Dark. Homicidally handsome. Educated. Successful. His list went on and on.

His chiseled jaw clenched tight as he looked over his pickings. With one hand in his jean pocket and the left hand out to show them that he was not married, he stood like a runway model awaiting one of the women to fall before him like a human offering. LaToya bet that Deana would be first.

They all blushed and said *hello* in unison, all accept LaToya. *Was it possible that he was actually coming over to say something to her*? He hadn't taken his gaze off her since he walked up.

She bit her bottom lip and waited. A shiver raced up her spine and caused goose bumps to form on her bare arms.

"LaToya, I'd like to introduce you to Mitch. He's a colleague of mine," Byron said, putting his hand on the attractive white man's shoulder. He looked at his friend with pride.

"Hi, Mitch," LaToya said blushing.

"Hello, LaToya, it's nice to meet you," Mitch said with a thick accent.

Great. Two hotties, she thought to herself.

Mitch was breathtaking as well. His green eyes sparkled but not with the same mischief as Byron's. There was something else looming in his unwavering gaze. His tanned face was framed by dark curly locks with a few streaks of distinguished gray, heavy arched eyebrows, light sprinkles of freckles across his straight nose and a clever charm that radiated from his bright smile. His wide, full lips were curved into a kiss above a dimpled chin. *But in all of his undeniable outward beauty, could it be that he was shy?*

She found that normal. White men tended to be tighter-lipped around black women here. And that was probably smart. The women at this table were like vultures.

Chuckling under her breath at the thought, she inadvertently made eye contact with *him*.

He smiled back as if understanding her sudden amusement. This time his look was different. Curious.

LaToya was speechless, and so were the rest of the girls.

So, did this man want to talk to LaToya? Had she finally landed one?

Byron's voice boomed, "I was just telling Mitch what a hell of a job you've done with my place, LaToya. You see, even though he's a great architect, he's one *lousy* house keeper. So, I was wondering if you might...consider taking him on as a new client?"

"Yes, I really need some help," Mitch said, fishing out his wallet. He pulled out his crisp, white business card and passed it to her.

All the women melted over his accent. Irish? Scottish?

Bryon picked up on the unspoken question. "Mitch originally hails from Dublin, hence the horrible accent. He just moved here about a year ago from our New York office, and he still hasn't gotten into the *Arizona* swing of things."

"Living here takes some getting used to." LaToya took the card and looked at it blankly. *Why did she get her hopes up anymore?* She would have been thrilled to have Bryon interested in more than just her *cleaning services*, but she would have settled for the white boy just to save face.

LaToya's friends looked down, embarrassed for her. They all thought that she had finally found a prospect for the bed; instead, she'd just picked up a possible prospect for her business. It was somewhat comical in a way. History continued to repeat itself for the poor girl.

"Okay, Mitch," she said, trying to hide her sudden disgust. "I'll give you a call tomorrow." She looked back up at him and sighed. Pain pulled at the sides of her nearly quivering mouth.

"Sounds wonderful. I actually have guests coming soon. So, I'll pay extra if you can fit me in ASAP," Mitch said eagerly.

LaToya smiled and put the business card in the pocket of her purse. She was relieved when Angela suddenly returned from the dance floor on cue, sweaty and drunk. Still laughing, she nearly fell over the men when she tried to sit down.

Bryon turned to Angela with a different look. His smile was much bigger now. Evidently, he had found his prize. Catching her in his strong grip as she nearly fell into him, he laughed.

"Are you okay?" he asked, touching her a little more than he had to.

"Great...now," Angela answered. She looked up into his eyes and swallowed hard. A suggestive look passed between the two. Sparks flew and suddenly the rest of the group was dim.

The queen of the ball had officially arrived. Angela was always the center of attention. Her fair skin, bright brown eyes, long *real* hair and a body from hell commanded attention not only from men but also from women. It had been as such for the entirety of her privileged existence.

The attention quickly turned from the awkward moment with LaToya to the tipsy beauty in front of them. In honesty, she was grateful. She could feel the pity emanating from around the table. Instead, she preferred for people to ignore her. It was better than being the central focus of a misunderstanding. *Case in point, the white guy.* Raising her eyebrow, she looked down at her now watered down drink and wished the night away.

However, even as she sat silently brooding, she felt Mitch still looking at her. She tried to glance away. *What did he want now? A babysitter? A nurse? Ugh. Men,* she thought as Angela giggled again.

Chapter Two

Early morning came quickly. LaToya pulled herself out of her full-sized bed and leaned over the side. Hitting the alarm on her I-pod clock radio, she snuggled her feet into her furry, pink slippers and made her way to the bathroom. Hair in a bun, she turned on the shower and grabbed her toothbrush.

On her mirror was a huge yellow note. LOSE 30 POUNDS! Looking up at the Post-It, she brushed her teeth in circular rotations as the dentist had instructed and shook her head. That note had been there for two months and since then, she had put on *three* pounds. The thought was depressing.

An hour later, she was at the Redmond's home with her cleaning crew preparing their house for a party that weekend and cleaning up from a party the night before.

Some people loved the social scene, and that number most definitely included the Redmond's. They were a strange but happy couple. Two cosmetic surgeons who had a flare for the eccentric and knew everyone who was anyone in Phoenix, the Redmond's were also one of her best clients.

It was a beautiful day outside. Around the pool, as she stuffed plastic plates and glasses into a huge, black garbage bag, she looked up at the blue sky and felt completely at peace. Life was good for her outside of being a lonely, young hag. She had a small business that was thriving, a small home that she loved, and friends and family who loved her. Plus, an hour ago, Barnes and Noble had called her and said that her new order of books had arrived. She couldn't wait to pick them up, get home and start her latest crime/romance series. It was almost like a hot date. In fact, it was a date.

Her employee, Marie, walked past her and smiled. LaToya snapped out of her daze and got back to work. She would think of her *date* later.

After the house was cleaned and the van had been loaded by the crew, she saw them off and headed to lunch. It was then that she thought about the embarrassing night before and the Irish fellow, Mitch. Mitch! Shit! She was supposed to call him back.

Still driving, she reached over into her purse on the passenger seat and felt through her well-organized pockets to find Mitch's card.

Money was money. She dialed him quickly on her Bluetooth and listened to the phone ring. Preparing to leave a message, she was shocked when he picked up.

"Hello," an Irish accent greeted.

"Mitch."

"Yes."

"It's LaToya from last night."

"Oh, wonderful. Good to hear back from you, LaToya."

"Good to talk to you as well. After meeting you last night, I am following up to see if you are still interested in hiring my cleaning service."

"Yes, very much."

"Great. When would be a good time to come by and assess your home needs?"

"Now, *actually*. I've just arrived back, and I'll be here for a while. Is right now a good time for you?"

"Sure."

"Okay. I'm in Scottsdale in Sonoran Hills off the 01 loop. Go to N. Scottsdale Road to East Adobe. I'm on Manana Drive. Do you know where that is?"

"I can find it. I have another client not far from there."

"Great. Well, I'll text you my exact address, and I'll see you in a bit."

"Alright, I'll be there in about 30 minutes."

LaToya made a u-turn in the street and headed east.

She had two ways at looking at last night. She could whine about being the odd one out *again*, or she could use every opportunity to get a new client. Honestly, she preferred the cleaning contract. While her friends were off getting laid, she'd be getting rich.

***

Thirty minutes later, LaToya pulled up in a winter green Mini-Cooper to the private drive of Mitch O'Keeffe. It was tranquil, upscale split-level situated on a hill in the middle of the community. She parked and went to the front door. Before she could ring the bell, Mitch opened it.

"LaToya," he said, happy to see her. Stepping aside, he motioned for her to come in. "Wasn't too hard to find, I hope."

"No, I just locked the address into my GPS," she said, stepping inside. Her feet echoed on the tile floor.

He stepped outside the door and looked at her car. "I love those things. Did you have yours customized?"

"Wouldn't have it any other way," she said, looking around. She ignored his small talk. *How big of mess did he have for her*?

Mitch closed the door and walked behind her. "So, do you want to walk around and take a look?"

"Do you mind?"

"No, not at all." He clasped his hands together. "Would you like something to drink? I have soda, water, beer..."

"No, I'm fine." She walked slowly through the large corridor and checked out the many large rooms piled high with unopened boxes.

Good grief, she thought to herself. *This place is a wreck.*

"And you say that you've been here a year?" she asked, taking out a notepad and pen.

"Yes. When I first arrived here, I had a crazy work schedule that I just assumed would calm down at some point. Needless to say that it never did."

"So you want my team to go through all the boxes too?" She scribbled something on her pad.

He looked at her hands. "No, some of those boxes are going to be picked up soon. My ex is coming to get them in the next couple of days."

LaToya looked back at him. He had a pained looked on his face. It must have been a touchy subject, but she had to find out what exactly he wanted.

"I can have *those* boxes out in the garage by the time that you're ready to start the process, if she fails to collect them. It'll just be my things in here by the time that you start."

"Okay." She put her foot on the first step of his wooden stairwell and looked back at him for approval.

"Please, go on," he urged.

His eyes told her that he had a very uneventful life. Most single men had places that they didn't want the cleaning service to invade. They would always walk her through each room, scanning it first for inappropriate objects like panties, dildos, porno. If they spotted something, they would immediately grab it up and stuff it away for later. Only later, she would get the contract and find it anyway. She had just about seen everything since she started her business. However, Mitch let her meander around alone. *Yep, uneventful.*

As she made her way up the crowed staircase, she noticed that he kept averting his eyes to the front door.

Holding on to the stairwell banister, she looked down curiously at him. *Was he trying something?*

"Are you waiting for someone?" she finally asked.

"Yes, but she won't be here until 3:45," he explained. "We've got plenty of time."

"Alright."

LaToya went up the stairs and looked around at each of the disheveled rooms. The huge master bedroom was basically an office with a bed in it, piled high with papers and coffee cups, blueprints and binders. The guest bedroom down the hall had been turned into a home gym, and the last bedroom was locked. She twisted the doorknob and then let go. Maybe this was his private place. Every man had one. There was no telling what was inside. *And she didn't want to know.*

She looked at the bathrooms, the game room and the study and then came back downstairs. He was still standing in the same spot with his brown, leather boot propped up behind him on the wall.

"Are there any other rooms?" She asked looking at his foot.

He quickly removed it like an admonished child and looked at the small dirt mark it left on the satin-finished paint. "Yes, there are more down each hall," he said, bending down to wipe the mark. Realizing it would need more care than a touch, he finally raised back up and guided her to the main hall. "The living room, dining room, uh, the kitchen are down this corridor. It's a real monster in the kitchen, by the way. And the den and the media room are down the other corridor along with a guest bathroom and a few closets and what not."

She walked behind him, watching his every move. He seemed nervous, which was typical for new clients. No one ever really liked having someone in his or her home.

After quickly looking through the other rooms with him, she finally made her way to his disheveled kitchen, where she sat down at the paper-covered table and pulled a contract from her backpack.

He sat down across from her with a cup of coffee and put the white porcelain to his lips.

"And this gets me services three times a week?" he asked, still looking down at the paper.

"Yes." Her voice was calm and soothing. She averted her eyes away from his mouth. "And you can decide on having a team to come in and clean it once and one person to keep it up on a regular basis, or you can pay to have a team of three to come in three times a week on a regular basis. The team is obviously more expensive but also quicker. It's really dependent upon your own preferences."

"Oh, I don't need all of that. The team can come once, and then the main person can come three times a week," he laughed nervously. "I'm not rich."

I can't tell, she thought to herself. "I understand," she said, pulling out a shiny, silver pen. It was her lucky closing pen, responsible for countless contracts. She'd had it since she started her business.

"Who will come in three times a week? And can I get a background check on them?" he asked.

"More than likely it will be me. I'll come in for about 2 hours, three times a week. Once we get the house under control, it will drop to an hour. But I have to be honest, Mr. O'Keeffe..."

He looked up from the paper quickly. His emerald eyes sparkled. "Please, call me Mitch."

"Okay, *Mitch*. It's going to take a lot of work to get your place up to par."

"I know." He scratched his head. "It's sort of embarrassing how horrid this place is."

Not as embarrassing as last night, she said inwardly. "I assure you that I've seen a lot worse. And yes, I will give you my information so that you can perform a background check."

"Well, if it's you then..." He didn't finish his sentence, but he did give her an approving smile, warm with true sincerity. Taking the pen, he signed the contract quickly and sighed. "Thank you for this, LaToya. I really appreciate your help. You don't know how much I need some *organization* in my life." He placed the pen down beside him and smoothed out the white paper.

"Well, I appreciate your business. And that's what my service is here for...to make your quality of life better," she said, hearing the doorbell ring.

"Speaking of quality of life," he said with a low growl. Standing up from the table, he never took his eyes off her. "Would you please excuse me for a moment? I have to see my son out to my ex-wife, or she'll think I'm procrastinating on purpose." His voice was low.

"Sure," LaToya said, putting the pieces together. *His ex. The locked door.* His kid had been upstairs.

Nodding at her, he stuffed his balled-fists into his pants pockets and strode out of the room in a slow mope.

About fifteen minutes later, as LaToya sat curiously and patiently waiting, she heard a door slam loudly. The bang made her sit up in the chair. *What the hell*, she thought to herself. *I hope I'm not getting into any mess.*

Shortly after, Mitch walked back into the kitchen with his head down. Instead of coming to sit at the table, he walked directly over to the kitchen island and planted his large hands on the cool ceramic tile beside a pile of blueprints and coffee mugs. Swallowing hard those words of disgust that sat at the tip of his tongue, his bulging Adam's apple moved under the weight of his frustrated reflex.

LaToya thought he looked as if he wanted to hit something. Clearing her throat, she motioned towards the contract. "Is this a bad time?" she finally asked. "I can always come back."

"No. No." His voice was solemn. It was apparent that he was pained terribly. He tried to recover from an obvious argument. In a quick motion, he turned to her and folded his large arms in front of him. His bulky muscles tightened under the thin plaid shirt. "I took my son to the dentist earlier, and he asked me on the way back to the house why me and his mom were getting divorced. When I tried to explain, he got upset and locked himself in his room. I imagine that it must be really difficult for him to understand."

"How old is he?"

"Nine," he answered with a small grin. "And big for his age."

"Any siblings?"

"No, we never got to that." He forced a smile to lighten his mood or at least lighten his brooding features, but she could see his sadness. It was apparent as the wedding ring that he wore. Catching her glancing at his hand, he shifted in his stance. "Enough about me. I'm sure that you don't want to hear *my* problems." He walked back to her. The chair screeched against the tile floor as he pulled it from under the table. "Let's talk about how this cleaning service can help me begin to get my life back."

With a comforting nod, she passed him the service documents.

Chapter Three

LaToya looked at the scale and cursed. Four more pounds? Ridiculous! Stepping down, she slipped on her robe and moped into the kitchen. What should she fix for breakfast? She wanted scrambled eggs and bacon, butter-covered pancakes and coffee, but she settled for dry toast and a boiled egg. It was enough to make her gag. Losing weight was like trying to get laid, virtually impossible for her.

Loading into her car after she was fully dressed, she pulled out of her garage and dropped the top to her Mini-Cooper. *Ah, there are some joys to life*, she thought. The dry wind blew through her curly, long braids, and the sun soaked into her skin, making her feel alive. Hidden behind black shades, she turned up Erica Badu on her radio and sang along in a horrible octave that made her laugh.

At the stop light, she glanced over to the passenger seat and eyed the *black bag*. In it were her dreaded running shoes and workout clothes. It sat there every day, and nearly every day it went untouched. But today, she planned to use it as soon as she finished the O'Keefe house. There was something in the air, something that made her feel good, and she was going to channel that energy into a workout that would burn some calories and shrink her waist. But first, she was headed to the see the *Irishman*.

Three weeks had passed, and the clean up was going quite well. Mitch didn't lie when he said that he worked a lot. With his son always gone and his mind focused on some *major* project that had him locked inside his bedroom, the house was mostly empty.

Normally, she would come in mid-day, turn on the television and watch soaps while she cleaned or listen to audio books on her I-phone. In fact, she was close to dropping him down to one hour three times a week, so that she could fit in another client to ease the workload on her other staff.

When she arrived to the house, as usual the place was empty. Putting away the keys, she set down the cleaning baskets and turned off the alarm.

"Mitch?" she called out. "Are you here?"

There was no answer.

Feeling extra giddy, she decided against watching soaps today. Instead, she slipped her buds into her ears and pushed play. She would settle for listening to her newest crime novel while she worked. At the moment, she was craving action and adventure. *The Medlov Crime Family* series would fit her need perfectly.

Setting her watch to a timer of exactly 60 minutes, she picked the baskets back up and headed to the living room to start there and work her way through the house.

Evidently, Mitch had been in the scotch again, because there was a lonely half-filled tumbler by a chair in the corner across from the fireplace next to a book about *winning in the workplace.* Picking up the glass, she thought about her scale and the black bag. If she walked from one part of the house to the kitchen every time that she found a dish, could that be considered exercise?

Convinced that it could, she turned and headed to the kitchen. As the woman's voice in her ears spoke of dead bodies on the floor of an office building found by a security officer, she walked through the corridor into the kitchen and headed straight to the sink. Placing the glass beside a pile of dirty dishes left since after her last visit, she stopped and wondered if Mitch ever cleaned for himself. It would be a complete miracle to come in and not find coffee cups everywhere. Too engulfed in her thoughts to see, she didn't even notice there was someone in the room with her.

Turning around, she screamed a loud yelp when she saw Mitch leaning over in the refrigerator. He appeared soaking wet with a towel wrapped firmly around his lower waist, revealing rippling muscles that tore out of his abdomen.

Startled by her as well, he jumped up from his leaning position as his towel fell down to the tile floor, pooling around his ankles.

It couldn't have been in slower motion for LaToya. Her reaction to turn her head was stopped by her need to pull the ear buds from her ears. The woman's voice was adding to her complete confusion.

"Oh my, I'm so sorry," she said, covering her eyes finally and looking away. She nodded her head profusely and batted her eyes.

"I didn't...know you were here." He scrambled to the ground and quickly retrieved his white towel. With trembling fingers, he wrapped himself again as he walked. "So very sorry, Latoya!" His voice drifted off as he walked fast down the hall. She could hear his feet as they moved, patting against the tile.

Leaning against the counter, she shook her head. The pump of her blood through her veins pounded in her ears. The replay in her mind made her buck her eyes. *What in the hell was that?* Who knew that Mitch had a package like *that*? Muscles everywhere. A penis the size of... a package of cookie dough. Wow, he was beautiful. She nodded her head again. And he was deaf. How could he not hear her screaming his name earlier?

Getting herself together, she put away her I-phone and made a conscience note not to use her audio books ever again in this house. Then suddenly, she had a taste for cookies. She'd probably eat Nestle baked cookies for the rest of the week. Opening the refrigerator door, she looked inside.

By the time that she got upstairs to clean, Mitch was fully dressed. He sat in his bedroom at the desk with a pencil clenched in his mouth and another one behind his ear. The lamp beside him illuminated his damp, brown curly locks of hair and the mole on his neck.

She tapped her knuckles on the door and waved after she'd stared at him for a while. "Hey," she said softly.

"Hey." He smiled shyly.

"Sorry about that, Mitch. I'll do a better job of making my presence known in the future."

"My mistake, really," he said, turning around in his seat. He stood up and waved her inside. "Are you ready to clean in here?" He barely made eye contact.

"I'll come back. I know that you're working." She clung to the door entry.

"Are you kidding? I need a break. I've been at this for like twelve hours already." He extended his hands out, plated his fingers together and cracked his knuckles.

LaToya tried to avert her eyes away from his pants. His perfect muscular frame was always hidden under micro-plaid, long sleeve shirts, curled up to the elbows and khakis pants that hid his long, bow legs. While she could always tell that he had a body, she didn't know he had a *body*. She was impressed and depressed, having never had a man that looked like that before.

"I made you a peace offering," she said, pulling a plate of cookies that she'd just baked from behind her back.

"Did you?" He walked over to her. The smell of soap and cologne filled her nose as he approached.

He looked down at her and smiled only inches away from her. His green eyes warmed her heart. "I'm going to go and get another cup of coffee. Would you like one?"

"No, thank you," she said, taking her eyes off him. *Who was she kidding?*

"Alright," he said, taking a cookie from her plate. Tasting them, he brought attention to the perfect curl of his lips. "Umm," he said in a deep, erotic growl. "These are delicious."

She smiled and gazed back up at him, unable to help herself. He looked better than the cookies. Her heart skipped a beat. At the moment, he looked better than anything that she could think of.

"Thank you *very much*, LaToya." His voice was low and soft.

"You're welcome. Just keep your clothes on, okay."

"I'll remember that." Remembering himself, he stepped past her. "Sure you don't want some coffee?" He raised his brows.

She shook her head.

He looked down at the floor and smirked. "Well, I'd better leave you to it then." Excusing himself, he left her alone in the room.

As she went over to his nightstand to pick up his multitude of half-full coffee mugs, she noticed the divorce papers sitting under the light with a huge coffee ring on the front page.

Not your business, she thought to herself. Quickly, she turned to get back to work. Picking up a pile of clothes to take to the washroom, she wondered what type of woman would divorce a man like Mitch. He seemed nice and more importantly normal. His list of sexable qualities where numerous:

1. She loved his accent. It was like butter.
2. All words rolled off his tongue like a romantic French love song.
3. He was responsible. Every once in a while, she'd accidentally look at the bills that he left thrown on the desk. Never once was there a past due notice. That was one of her pet peeves. *If you could make the bill, you could pay it on time.*
4. He also never had a house full of people and had not once had a woman over. So, he wasn't a whore or a poor planner.
5. He was incredibly handsome.
6. He was a gentlemen.
7. He had a package from hell.
8. He seemed to be a good father.
9. He was ambitious.
10. He was easy to talk to.
11. And he was understanding

She put the dirty clothes in the hamper in the washroom and hit the dial for cold. Did it really matter how long his list was anyway? Mitch O'Keef was not interested in LaToya Jenkins. That she did know.

When she was done with the upstairs, she headed back downstairs to find Mitch at the kitchen table asleep.

Snoring lightly, he cradled his head in his arms with one hand still on his coffee cup. She knew that he had been working hard and felt a twinge of pity for the poor guy. A man of his age should be out enjoying himself, not spending every waken moment working or worrying. A smirk formed on her lips. *So should she for that matter.* As she moved the coffee cup, so he wouldn't knock it off the table, he stirred.

He looked up with tired eyes and smiled. "Thanks," he said stretching.

"No problem. Maybe you should go up and get some rest." Her hand rested on his massive back.

"I probably would, but I'm starving," he said, sitting up. He looked at his watch. "Are you finished for the day?" Peering back up at her, he raised his brow.

"Yep," she said, putting her gloves in her cleaning basket.

He eyed her. "Would you like to go and get something to eat?"

LaToya tilted her head. "I don't know. I don't normally..."

"Oh come on. You mean to tell me that you're not hungry?"

"Because I'm fat, I have to be hungry, huh?"

"Fat? You're not fat," he said, shaking his head. "You want to see a fat woman, you should see my grandmother. Now, there's a woman with a little extra meat on her bones. She's like 300 pounds and wears red polka dots to church every Sunday."

She laughed. So did he.

"So, will you please have an early dinner with a starving man? I don't think I've eaten in like three days, or will Mr. Jenkins or your boyfriend be terribly put off."

"There is neither."

"Well, then you can't possibly say no."

LaToya bit her lip. This was not professional, but he did look pitiful and what if he went to sleep at the wheel and killed himself? She could not afford to lose a client.

"It's just that I planned to go walking before dark," she explained. "So..."

"I've got an entire gym upstairs. You can use my treadmill when we get back."

"No. No, I can't," she shrugged her shoulders. "Okay. I'll have dinner with you, *but* it has to be short, and then I have to go workout *and* not in your gym."

"You are wonderful," he said, standing up. "Give me two minutes to grab my keys and my wallet and then we can go."

***

Four hours later, LaToya and Mitch were still out. The Tilted Kilt Irish pub was hidden in a thick of a chain of stores not far from Mitch's house. Evidently, when he did go out, this was his place of choice.

Covered in green walls, decorated with all
things Irish, paneled with dark wood and bubbling
over with Guinness beer, his hangout was as close
as she imagined he could get to something from
home.

A few people knew him there and a few others
wanted to know him. LaToya saw at least five
women staring at them from across the room.
Every time he'd catch someone's eye, that person
would lean over to their friend and nod their way.
However, Mitch just kept talking and laughing.
Either he did not care, or he did not care to show
that he cared.

Music played in the background, something
that sounded like an Irish jig, and people laughed
and whirled about. It was a lot less pensive than
the clubs she went to with her girls, but it was still
packed.

In the corner, a group of men threw darts, while
a group of women flirted a few feet away from them
shooting pool. The bar was full with every seat
occupied. Couples sat beside each other talking
and drinking, kissing and fighting.

The barmaids were dressed in red, kilt-like uni-
forms. Most of them weren't above a size four but
had breasts the size of bowling balls. They brought
cold beer fast and plates full of greasy foods to the
table every half hour, all the while bending over in
front of them so that Mitch might have a better
view. But he never looked once.

This entire thing was extremely out of character for her, and she berated herself silently for it as each hour passed. However, she was having a great time.

Mitch was funny. He didn't take himself too seriously, but he was passionate about two things - Zack and work. Zack was his son, mothered by a housewife gone rogue right after moving to Phoenix. Mitch had sworn the heat had driven her mad but inwardly, he knew it was Zach's pediatrician who had stolen her.

"Here's a spin on things," he said with his Timberland boots up on the booth seat across from him. "Most of the time they say that spending time with your family will keep you together and that's true, but keeping your son out of the pediatrician's office is the key." They both laughed. He shook his head and continued. "Zack's got chicken pocks, you say? Oh, we'll give him a little oatmeal cream for his body and send him on his way, *but whatever you do,* don't send him to the doctor...he'll come back with an ointment and the wife comes back pregnant."

LaToya stopped laughing. *Wow. That was deep.* He looked at her and nodded as if to say, *yes, that's what happened. That was my fall from grace.* She understood and felt compelled to share as well.

"I was engaged once," she said, barely above a whisper. She smiled as she confessed. "He was a great guy, *so I thought.* We planned this great wedding, and then I found him in the bed with one of my closest friends." Running her straw around in the nearly empty mug of beer, she looked away from him. It was still painful for her. "They're happy now. They have three kids and live in San Diego, where I'm from."

"Oh, so you're not from here?"

"Nope. I left home after that and started my cleaning business."

"Well, I can't blame you. If I didn't have a child with Elaine, I would quit my job and hightail it out of here, too. Do you know how embarrassing it is for everyone to know that your wife has run off with the pediatrician?"

"Yeah, trust me, I feel your pain. I've been embarrassed on a few occasions."

"Like when?" He took another sip and looked at the straw sticking out of her mug. *Who drank beer out of a straw?*

"Outside of the engagement thing?"

"Yeah, purge. Go on. It's good for me."

"Good for you?" she laughed.

"Yeah, it helps me feel less worthless."

She laughed. "The night I met you, I thought...no, not just me, everyone thought that you were coming over to ask me to dance or ask me out or ask me anything other than to clean your house."

Mitch bucked his eyes. "Is that why you had that look on your face?"

"What *look*?"

"Like you were repulsed. Like I had a booger in my nose."

"I wasn't repulsed," she laughed.

"Well, you sure *seemed* repulsed. I was glad that Byron made my attentions clear. You seemed relieved afterwards. You were like..." He swallowed and lightened his voice. "Please, please don't let the white boy ask me out, especially standing there with a huge booger in his nose." He stuck a fried pickle in his mouth.

"I wasn't relieved, and you didn't have a booger in your nose."

"No?" He tilted his head. Licking his fingers, he winked at her. "You seemed relieved."

LaToya lied. "Well maybe just a little bit."

They both laughed again. The tension broke.

"I don't imagine that many women would find me worthy right now. I've just received the final divorcee decree to a woman that I'm now paying child support to for *two* children."

"Two?"

"She had the *other* one while we were married. Then I signed the birth certificate, so by law the pediatrician's kid is mine," he winced.

"Oww. It keeps getting worse for you," LaToya said, raising her finger to get the check.

"Yes. I'm currently fighting it in court. Do you want another beer?" he asked.

"No, I'm not Irish. This is bordering on illegal."

"We passed *illegal* about three hours ago, my dear." He looked at his watch. "You know, if we were back in New York, we could walk home from this place."

"Yes, but here it wouldn't be a good idea."

"I know." He drank the last of his beer and turned to her. "So why did your ex marry that woman? I can't rightly understand it after hanging out with you."

"Because she was prettier and smaller than me. I was always a big girl. I still am for that matter. I've always been a little bigger than most of my friends."

His green eyes bulged a little. "Big? You're robust, but you're not fat. I mean, I like a woman with a little meat on her bones."

"Well, I have a lot of meat." She sucked down on the straw.

He leaned over and looked at her legs hidden under black tights and a black, long, form-fitting shirt. Sweeping her body once more, he raised his brow and winked at her.

LaToya was leaning with her hands cupping her chin. She watched him eye her up and down and then rolled her eyes. He had to have a motive for looking at her like that. If he thought that he was going to get free cleaning services because the wife may be taking half of his stuff, he had another thing coming.

He finally spoke. "You're *weight* is in all the right places, LaToya. That's what matters. Any man who thinks otherwise is an idiot. You have to have something to hold onto at night. I'm sure you make a gentleman feel warm, like there is nowhere else to be in the world but in your arms."

"Okay, you've had enough to drink," she said finally. *What else was there to say?* He'd nearly made her choke on his words. If she stayed, she might do something stupid. Shaking her head, she tried to put it all into perspective. *Give the man a break. He's been drinking,* she said to herself.

"Are you attracted to white men?" he asked abruptly. He swallowed hard after his question and sat his mug on the table. She watched his Adam's apple bulge. His eyes were bright. Could it be that he was sincere?

"I'm not attracted to any man on the rebound, Mitch," she said sympathetically. "Are you cute? Yes. You're probably everything that a woman needs, but you just came out of a serious relationship, a marriage rather and..."

"Goodness, woman. I just asked if you were attracted to white men. I didn't ask you to be my *girl*," he said, shaking his head.

There was complete silence.

"Are you ready?" she asked, getting out of the booth.

"Yeah," he said, under his breath. Standing up, he threw the money down on the table and watched her walk off. "Must have been something I said."

When LaToya and Mitch arrived back at his place, she parked the car and turned down the radio. Although it was just a short drive, he had fallen back to sleep with his head tilted back on the seat. Softly, she placed her hand on his and stirred him awake.

"We're here," she smiled.

"Wow, I went to sleep that quickly?" He sat up and yawned. "Thanks for...everything."

"Welcome."

He paused for a minute. "Look, if I did anything to make you feel uncomfortable, I do apologize. It was very nice of you to take time out of your day for me. I needed it, and you didn't have to."

She cut him off with the wave of her hand. "You didn't offend me. I'm a big girl, trust me."

Mitch nodded.

"Look, your home is to the point where we can go to one hour three times a week now," she explained.

He frowned. "I *did* offend you."

"No. No. I was going to tell you earlier, but then all this happened, and it really just slipped my mind. Don't you see the difference in your place?"

"It looks great. I feel like I can actually think in there. My work productivity has gone up tremendously because of you."

She liked that. "Well, I'll see you Friday...for one hour then."

"Alright...goodnight."

But the hand he had on the door didn't move. Instead, he looked at her, as if he was waiting for something. LaToya watched his face, how beautiful he seemed, how different he was becoming in her mind.

Mitch swallowed hard again. LaToya was an enigma to him. She was strong and silent, direct and professional, but there was a side to her that he was curious to see. Earlier, she had smiled and laughed with him, shared with him. He had forgotten all about Elaine. For one moment, he was just a normal guy out with a beautiful girl grabbing a bite to eat. And now, something deep inside of him wanted to know more about her.

"Rebound," she finally said, breaking his concentration on the beautiful curl of her glossy lips.

"Excuse me?"

"It's all a part of the rebound," she said as she hit the console and unlocked the doors. "Goodnight, Mitch. Get some rest."

Chapter Four

LaToya laid in bed past the alarm's loud blare on Thursday. Staring at the ceiling, she thought about Mitch *again*. He was an odd ball. To look at him, she would have sworn that he had it all together. He had a great house, a great job and a great body. But looks where not everything and mostly they were deceiving. He was also funny and warm, very much aware of his shortcomings and amazingly, there wasn't a conceited bone in his body. He was quite an unusual package.

The smell of his cologne came to mind, and she trailed her fingers over the comforter and bit her lip. What if she had taken him up on his advances? What if she had moved in just close enough to kiss his lips last night? Would she be alone in her bed right now?

It had been a long time since she was in a relationship. After the breakup with Troy four years ago, all things sexual had gone out the window, *maybe except her toys*. Her move from San Diego to Phoenix had been sudden. She followed Angela to this desert oasis in hopes of starting over. When she first bought her little two-bedroom home, she had sworn to lose weight, change her entire outer appearance from her hair to her makeup to her style. But nothing had changed except her view of men.

Dates had been sparse since she arrived in Phoenix. She'd gone on two, in fact, in the last year. Both were disasters. One man picked his teeth throughout the entire date and the other talked about his Porsche through dinner, which once he walked her to the car, she found out was an '83 in horrible condition and missing paint spots on the hood.

   After two blind catastrophes, she decided that dating was not her thing and spent all of her time either at home or with her friends.

   Today, she decided to take the day off work. Instead of going to Byron's place and cleaning, she sent one of her other cleaners. She was going to relax and clean her own place for a change before her friends came over for dinner. While it was not eventful, it would definitely be enjoyable. She hadn't seen them in a month and was curious to see what new developments had taken place in every-one else's life.

   Pulling herself out of bed, she went into the bathroom and got on the scale. Looking down at the machine as it populated on the digital reader, she gasped when she saw the number. Quickly, she dropped her robe. Still not happy with the number, she took off her watch and earrings. As she looked down at the number again, she finally gave up.

***

   Sitting around the fire pit in LaToya's perfectly manicured backyard, the women laughed and drank wine while she served them up a quick meal and turned on the lanterns. The night was ending, and now was the time to dish the dirt as customary for their small clan.

"So, tell us what happened with Byron," Deana said to Angela as she crossed her feet Indian style.

Angela grinned and looked over at LaToya, knowing she was the only one of her friends who hadn't heard the news.

"Well," Angela answered, pulling her hair behind her ear. "He and I had dinner again for the *second* time last night."

"And," Kristen pushed. "How did it go?"

"It was so romantic. After a great dinner, he took me back to his place and fixed me a nightcap. Then we sat by the fireplace and kissed all night."

"All you did was kiss?" Kristen asked disappointed.

"Among other things," Angela laughed. She raised her brow. "He has big feet, big fingers and big...everything else."

"Bryon's got a big penis!" Deana laughed. "So, he *does* have everything. Damn, I wish he had asked me out that night. I could use a good man, with a good job and no children. He almost seems unreal."

LaToya sat down with them and sipped her wine. Blushing for them, she thought about her client and nodded her head. She had guessed that about Byron. She couldn't even name how many times she had thought about him and how attractive he was, but she knew that she wasn't his type. It was a lost cause.

"Well, I'm glad that I could introduce you two," LaToya said chiming in.

"I'm glad you did, too, girl. Good looking out. " Angela rubbed LaToya's leg. "He's wonderful or something like it. The only thing I don't like is his work schedule. He works all the time."

"I know. So does Mitch," LaToya said quickly.

The circle became quiet, and suddenly only the crackle of the fire could be heard.

"Mitch?" Angela looked over at LaToya. "The white boy from the club?"

"Oh, he's a client now. Remember? That was the entire reason for him even coming over," LaToya explained. "And he's always working when I'm there."

"Uh huh," Kristen said laughing. "She *has* been glowing all day."

"I have not," LaToya scoffed. "He's a nice enough guy. He's just had a hard time since he's been here."

"Well, maybe you should help him out," Deana joked. "Cook that brother a meal. Wait for him to get off work and be in his bed naked with a bottle of lube and a bowl of cherries."

"No," LaToya laughed. "He doesn't like me that way. He's just a client. I mean, true we did go out for drinks last night but..."

The circle erupted in happy laughter.

"This bitch has been holding out on us all night! You didn't tell us that you had a man," Deana cackled.

"You know I hate when you use *that* word," LaToya admonished.

"And she's blushing," Angela pointed out. "She's been seeing the w*hite boy* and didn't want her girls to find out."

"No," LaToya shrugged the notion off. "He doesn't like me like that."

"Are you sure?" Kristen asked.

"Why would he?" LaToya shook her head. "I'm not his type. He probably is attracted to little, bitsy, blonde, blue-eyed, prissy..."

"Not all men want that, LaToya," Deana said.

"How would you guys know? Neither of you are above a size eight. I'm fighting to stay in a 14. Shit, I've gained five pounds in the last month."

"Well, have you been working out?" Angela asked. "I keep telling you to come with me to the gym. If you want a man, girl, you're going to have to get rid of some of that weight. It blocks them from seeing you. Men with money don't date big women. That's probably the only thing that is keeping you two from hooking up."

"I don't have time," LaToya said, uncomfortable about talking about her size. "And if a man can't like me for me, then I don't want him."

"No man likes you for just you. He likes you because you look a certain way, cook a certain way, screw a certain way, make a certain wage...you feel me?" Deana said, taking a large gulp of wine from her glass.

"Look, if you like him, then you need to do what it takes to get him," Kristen added, pouring another glass of wine. "It's not that much weight. Get lipo. I know you have the money."

"And once you drop the weight, then you'll get the man for sure," Angela agreed.

"He doesn't like me," LaToya said softly. She really wished that they would all shut up.

"Did he tell you he didn't like you?" Deana asked.

"No," LaToya put her glass to her lips. "I just know."

***

In the tranquil silence of her backyard after her friends had left and everything had been cleaned, LaToya sat in her lawn chair with her feet propped up and looked up at the full moon and the incandescent stars. Life was peaceful again now that she was alone. It was strange how accustomed she had become to being in solitude and how relaxed she was with that fact.

Her mother always worried that she would grow old alone. After the break-up, she had begged her to stay in San Diego and not run from her life. There was one problem for LaToya in doing that. If she stayed, she knew that she'd never really heal from her broken heart. Plus, her mother was married, her sisters were married, even her brother was married. Everything was just a constant reminder of what she did not have. At least now, all though she did have the occasional lonely night and sad moments during holidays, she enjoyed her life and what she had chosen to do with it.

Looking at her watch, she decided that it was time to get to bed. Morning would come soon for her and while she did take the day off to relax, she was quite certain that she would make up for it tomorrow.

Going into her perfectly clean, all-white bath-room, she turned the silver, shiny knobs on her garden bathtub and lit her vanilla candles. She was just about to grab her towels when she noticed the light blinking on her phone. One missed call.

She checked it to find that Mitch had called. She dialed him back quickly, sure that he was just checking to make sure that she would come the next day.

"Hi Mitch, you called?"

"Yes, I did. How are you?"

"Fine." She avoided the small talk.

"Good. Look, this is really a big favor that I have to ask, but I have a meeting tomorrow that is *really* important, and it's scheduled during the time that my ex wife is bringing Zach over. Can you stay with him until I arrive by any chance?" His voice pleaded.

"Mitch, that's not my job."

"I know. I know. Trust me. It just that I don't really have anyone else, and if I give her any leeway with my visiting times, I won't see him all weekend.

And I just can't bear to have him spend *my* time with *the pediatrician*."

"Mitch's it's not professional for me to go from cleaning service to babysitter..."

"I'm not asking from one professional to another. I'm asking you as a friend. Please, Latoya," he begged.

LaToya rolled her eyes and sighed. Shifting her weight from one foot to another, she crossed her arms. "Just this once."

"Thank you. Thank you so much," he said relieved. "I'll make this up to you. I promise."

"The way to make it up to me is to never put me in this position again."

"I won't. But thanks. You're saving my ass."

"Goodnight, Mitch."

"See you tomorrow."

LaToya hung up the phone and shook her head. *What was she getting herself into?*

***

One o'clock on the dot, LaToya arrived at the O'Keefe house with cleaning baskets in tow. Opening the door of the house, she sat her supplies down and turned off the alarm, then made her way to the kitchen. On the island table was a note from Mitch thanking her for the *favor* and promising to make it up to her. *She doubted that he could.*

Well after the last room had been cleaned, the doorbell rang. *Just on time*, she thought, *at least the little bugger didn't interrupt me before I finished cleaning.* With the click of the remote, she got up from the couch and made her way to the front door. As she approached, she could see a woman's shape behind the stain glass window and a child beside her peering inside with his hands firmly placed on the glass. *Ugh, I just cleaned those*, she thought.

LaToya turned the knob slowly, dreading for some reason meeting Mitch's ex-wife. As the door opened and the hinges creaked, the woman on the other side stood smiling and ushered her son inside. With his luggage in tow, she stopped in the foyer, refusing to go any further into her old home.

You must be LaToya," the woman said, extending her hand. "Hi. I'm Elaine."

LaToya was lost for words. His ex-wife. His baby's mother. His heart breaker was a black woman. Her hair was pulled back in a soft, short amber ponytail.   Her features were fair lending to the possibility that she was multiracial with her slim nose and thin lips, but more than anything, Elaine was black. LaToya tried to repress her smirk.

"Hi, Elaine.   I'm LaToya...the cleaning lady. Mitch asked me to stay for a while and watch your son until he arrives."

Elaine shifted her Gucci purse on her shoulder and looked back for her son, who had quietly made his way up the stairs to his room.

She stumbled over her words and spoke softly. "Mitch said that you were a *friend*. He didn't say that you were his cleaning lady." She smirked. "For a moment, I have to admit, I was jealous." Elaine actually seemed relieved.

LaToya chuckled. "Well, I'm a friend, too...I guess." She frowned.

Elaine nodded. "Regardless, thank you for doing this for him. Felix and I are going on a small road trip and if Mitch hadn't had someone to watch Zach then he would have had to go with us."

"Oh. I understand. No, it's no problem." LaToya stood in her place, confused but enlightened.

"If you need anything, I've written my numbers here." She proudly passed *Dr. Felix Hampstead's* card to LaToya with her numbers written on the back in red ink.

"Thank you." LaToya took the card and smiled again. "I'm sure that we'll be fine."

"Okay then." Elaine laughed nervously. "Well, it was nice meeting you, but I best be off. I'm way behind schedule." She made her way to the entrance.

With a small nod, LaToya closed the door behind Elaine and then turned to look past the foyer at the stairs. Should she go up there and see if the little guy was hungry? Should she ignore him?

A thought crossed her mind. It probably wasn't smart to ignore a nine year old. If he got into trouble of some sort, she would be responsible, because stupidly, she'd gotten herself involved.

Hiking up the stairs, she went to the room at the end of the hall and knocked on the door. The television was already blasting.

"It's open," the boy said dryly.

LaToya opened the door and found Zach in front of his television playing his Wii.

"Hey," LaToya said, leaning against his desk.

"*Hey* is for horses," he said, without looking up.

"Well some *hey* is for trying to be nice to little kids who don't introduce themselves when they meet an adult." She raised her brow at him.

Zach looked up. His eyes were the same color as his father's, a deep, tranquil green. His skin was only slightly kissed by the sun giving him a permanent and beautiful tan and his cheeks were rosy red. He was tall for his age and bordering on pudgy. Curly masses of black hair topped his head, and he wore plaid like his father and a pair of dark khakis. He looked just like the many pictures of him on the walls throughout the house. Only before knowing who his mother was, LaToya just attributed Zach's color to something other than melanin.

"*Hello*, I'm Zachary," he said, turning from his toy. "What's your name?"

"LaToya Jenkins. I'm a friend of your dad's."

"I've heard that before." He turned and started to play the game again. "Are you and my dad getting married? Are you going to have a baby or something like mom and Felix?" He kept his eyes on the television.

LaToya shook her head. "No, I clean his house. Good grief." She tried not to sound surprised considering what she knew the boy had gone through.

Zach didn't respond.

"Are you hungry or something? If you are, I can fix you something to eat. Otherwise, I'll leave you to your hypnotics, because you sort of freak me out."

"Can I have a sandwich?" he asked.

"Sure, let me see what your dad has. You wanna stop playing that and come downstairs for a minute." She motioned towards the door.

He put down the control on his entertainment cabinet. "What are hypnotics?" he asked, looking up at her under heavy eyelashes with a curious gaze.

"Those computer games put you in a state of um...oblivion about the world. You should try reading a book."

He walked beside her. "A book? You don't have kids, do you?"

"Nope. You can tell?"

"Yeah," he said, cracking his knuckles.

***

Right before dusk, tired mentally and physically, Mitch put his key in the front door of his home and opened it. As he entered the house and closed the door, he heard something that he had not heard in a long time. Laughter. It was his son and LaToya. Their voices blended to make a blissful melody of

happiness that rang through the halls. Unexpected-
ly, it sent goose bumps up his arm.   He hadn't
heard his son laugh like that in a long time. And
there was something else he hadn't had in a long
time.   The smell of food cooking in his kitchen,
emanating through his house like a fragrance of
pure love.

The glow of the sun setting in the horizon made
the house appear to be literally alive. The dancing
flickers of light beamed brightly through the
windows as its blaze faded into the distance. The
burnt yellow walls topped with white crown mold-
ing, decorated with beautiful art and low, receding
lights under expensive tile floors, adorned with
elegant furniture seemed like a real home tonight.
It was the first time that he felt like he had actually
walked into his life again. The house was clean.
His son was laughing. Food was cooking, and there
was a woman waiting for him after a long day at the
office.

Quietly, he put down his briefcase, dropped his
blueprints at the table in the foyer and walked
slowly down the hall, trying hard not to be detect-
ed. As he got closer, he heard his son asking
LaToya a question.

"So you've read it?" Zach asked.

"Yes," LaToya replied.

"Well, what happens? I've got an assignment in
class on *Moby Dick*. It's *supposed* to be a classic or
something, but if you ask me, it blows. No one

wants to read it. I want to read *Diary of a Wimpy Kid*, but Ms. Clementine won't let us."

"You *should* read Moby Dick. It *is* a classic. And if I tell you what happens, then you won't read it. And then you'll have missed out."

"I won't read it anyway," he joked. "Why don't they just make every book into movie? It's so much easier."

"Some books are better in print, Zach. I've seen the *Moby Dick* movie. It's lacking."

"What does that mean?"

"It's better on paper."

"No, it's not." He paused. "How many books have you read anyway?"

"Thousands."

"Thousands?" Zach asked in disbelief. His voice sounded exasperated at the thought. "Why?"

"Because," she hunched her shoulders and smiled. "I love to read."

LaToya didn't want to tell him that single people had to find a serious hobby to make up for the time that they weren't spending with a mate, and many like her preferred reading to get away from the life that they currently had to go to a place that they'd never been. It was one of her favorite hobbies. In fact, she had turned her spare bedroom into a full library, where she had collected over 2,000 books.

Mitch stood in the doorway watching the two as they talked. Zach sat on the island beside LaToya while she stood cutting up vegetables and preparing their meal. The two had only just met, but it seemed that they had known each other for a lifetime. Their chemistry was pleasant and easy, unlike how he'd seen his son with the pediatrician. Zach liked her. He liked her.

Dipping his head to hide the emotions that he was sure he wore on his tired face, he looked down at his brown boots to fight the pain of what he missed, what he longed for. He wanted someone there doing just what she was doing on a permanent basis, not cooking, not cleaning but nurturing. More than his son needed it. He needed it. It was such a shame that he had lost it not to being a cheat or a bastard, but by being a good man.

"Oh, you're home," LaToya said, looking his way. She cast a bright smile at him and waved her silver spatula. "Come help us. You can take the bread out of the oven while Zach sets the table."

Obediently, Zach jumped down from the island and went to the cupboard to retrieve the plates. "Hey dad," he said in a chipper tone.

"*Hello*, Zach," Mitch said, noting his son's ease with the English language today. Elaine was always so hard on him about his language skills. He had always thought the woman went overboard with her lectures on using *proper English*, especially when she set such bad examples for him in every other way.

LaToya raised her brow at him. Mitch looked great as normal. A statue of confidence. Even after working ten hours, he looked resilient and painfully handsome.

He went over to the stove, put on his mitten and pulled out fresh bread as she had instructed. The warm aroma lit up the kitchen. Setting it down on the oven, he looked over at LaToya and mouthed *thank you.*

"Welcome," she said, putting the cut veggies into the stew that she was cooking.

He stood beside her, almost arm-to-arm and refused to move. He liked being beside her. It made him stand taller.

"How was work?" she asked nonchalantly.

"Great," he answered with a grin. He hadn't been asked that in a while. Running his hand through his chocolate curls, he stopped at the top of his head and scratched it. The muscles in his arms protruded out, even in his red, plaid shirt. "How was your day with Zach?" he asked her, feeling his son looking at the two of them without turning around.

"Nice." She looked up at him and put down her utensils. "You have a very *sweet* son. He was easy to watch."

"I'm not sweet," Zach said as he set the table. He looked over at the pair with a stern glare.

LaToya grinned. "He's a man's man, huh?"

"Oh yeah," Mitch said, watching her cook. He liked the way that she moved around the kitchen. He liked the way that she moved period.

She picked the utensils up again and began to
stir her food carefully. Her body bent into the
stove, causing her behind to stick out. He looked.
Nice. Really nice.

Tasting the stew from her silver spoon, she
reached for a bottle of paprika and doused a little in
the pot. Mitch watched her mouth. He wondered
what it would be like to kiss her lips. He'd never
kissed a pair so full and inviting. Evidently, his
thoughts were a little too readable, because she
glanced up at him from the corner of her eye. Her
long lashes batted at him. He tried to redirect.
"You know how to get around a kitchen, don't
you?"

"I love to cook. Can't you tell," she said, scoot-
ing him out of her way. "Dinner will be ready in a
minute. Zach, go and wash up."

"Alright," he said, finishing the table. "There,
it's ready." He looked at the table proudly. It was
set for three tonight, instead of a lonely pair.
Tilting up on his tiptoes, he meshed his hands
together in complete satisfaction of his master-
piece.

Mitch looked at his son and nodded. "Good
job."

"Thanks. You too," the boy said with a clever
grin.

LaToya looked on quietly and felt a twinge of
pride herself. *It's the simple things that make a
family happy*, she thought to herself.

As soon as Zach ran out of the kitchen, Mitch turned to LaToya. There was a glimmer in his eye as if he was about to say something that might ruin everything. LaToya instantly recognized it. She side-stepped past him and went to the refrigerator to give him some space and to grab the butter.

She clenched the cool handle of the refrigerator door and looked blankly inside. "I'm not trying to win you over, Mitch. I'm just trying to be your friend," she said softly, shaking her head. Reaching inside, she grabbed the butter and closed the door.

A sly grin crossed his lips. "You're doing both, LaToya. You're my friend and something else, but I just can't place it yet." He reached over to the wine rack and pulled out a bottle of Chardonnay. Opening the bottle, he poured it carefully into a glass and passed it to her. She took it and leaned against the countertop across from him.

"That *other thing* would be your cleaning lady. Remember?"

"Outside of that." He winked at her. "You're something else to me. You're something else to this house."

She let a smile crack from the side of her full lips but quickly hid it by biting them. "You didn't tell me that you had a black wife."

Startled, he quickly gulped down his remaining wine. Without looking at her, he answered in a gruff tone, "I didn't think it was important." He poured another glass quickly. "And she's my *ex-wife*."

"I pegged you as having a petite little blonde for a wife."

"Really?" Mitch shook his head. "Everyone automatically assumed that when we were married. There would always be the shock and awe when I brought her to a dinner party with members from the firm. Then it would be quickly dismissed. You know. They would be like, *oh he's a foreigner. He doesn't know how things work.* But I'm not like that. I feel like I should be allowed to love who I want to love. No questions asked."

"I guess you got a lot of flack for it, huh?"

"Not as much flack as I did for her leaving me for the pediatrician."

The thud of the bottle against the granite tabletop made LaToya chuckle. He was still sensitive about that evidently. She moved on for now.

"I missed a client tonight. So, I'm charging you double," she said in a matter-of-fact tone.

"It's worth it. I'll pay triple." He didn't smile, but he gave her a wicked gaze. His green eyes raced her body in one suggestive sweep.

"Fine. I'll invoice you." She didn't smile but her eyes did. She took a sip of the wine and held the glass under her chin.

***

After dinner, Zach lazily made his way up to his room after giving LaToya a hug and thanking her for a delicious meal. They were all stuffed and ready to retire, including LaToya, who hadn't planned to stay so long. *Just like Mitch to keep me here another night with something*, she thought to herself.

Grabbing her cleaning baskets and backpack, she walked to the door with Mitch trailing closely behind her.

He watched her as she walked. Her sway was confident and seductive. Her hips were curvaceously full and led to a plump middle and long back. Her dark skin gave contrast to the pink t-shirt she was wearing. He looked at the nape of her neck and the curly hair that trailed from her braids pulled in a tight, perfect bun. Everything about her was delicate. Her almond shaped eyes, her careful chin, her high cheek bones, her perfectly unblemished, dark chocolate skin – it all made her face unique. The small diamonds sparkling in her ears brought more attention to the startling whites of her eyes, the perfect white teeth hidden behind full lips and the fine, conservative taste of a self-made woman.

As she got to the door, he reached for the knob but didn't open it. Looking down at her, into her warm, big brown eyes, he suddenly couldn't breathe. She was different. Everything about her was different from what he had known. She was so strong, so sure of herself, until it made him feel safe. *Wasn't he the man? Wasn't he supposed to have that type of effect on her?*

"Mitch, the door," she reminded, looking at his hand.

"Thanks again for tonight," he said in a low whisper, searching for the right words to say.

"You've said that about one hundred times. You *are* welcome." She smiled. It was becoming hard to even be short with him.

He opened the door slightly, then closed it and leaned against the entry so that she could not pass.

"If I attempt to kiss you, will you kick my ass?" he asked with a playful grin. His accent was thick now.

"Probably," she said sighing. "These baskets are sort of heavy. Just let me go home, Mitch. I'm tired. I told you what you're feeling is just the rebound..."

"Oh shut up with that, woman," he said quickly.

Leaning into her, he grabbed her arms quickly before she could protest and pulled her into him. Firmly, he held her warm body close to his and met her lips with a curious kiss, searching her warm, sweet, full mouth with his own. She tasted delicious, like a sweet, expensive delicacy. She tried to fight, tried to pry away, but she finally gave in. His cologne, his lips, his touch, it all released into her. She went limp, dropping the baskets on the floor beside them.

Mitch thought that she might try to hit him, but instead, she wrapped her strong hands around him. He could feel her nails trailing in his curly hair. She moaned. It was a frail cry of sensual pleasure that spoke to the deepest of his sexual desires.

The small recognition of her touch made him hard. He pressed against her, kissing her deeper, tasting more of her. Feeling her thick, full bosom against him, he lost himself in her mouth, in the fleshy feel of her minty tongue.

Sucking it, savoring it, he kissed her until he had made his point. When he released her, her beautiful eyes were still closed shut, covered by long lashes that curled over each other.

He swallowed hard and prepared to be slapped. However, when her eyes finally flitted open, she only licked her lips and took a deep breath.

LaToya thought of that great book, *Waiting to Exhale*. She thought of Terry McMillan when she opened her eyes. She felt like she was floating, like the sun had re-emerged in the middle of the night. His lips were still wet, still ready. She licked her own and felt a silky warmness between her hot thighs that caused her knees to shake.

"I'm certain that this is not a *rebound thing*. I...I just had to make that point clear. Now, can I carry your things to your car for you since they are heavier tonight than usual?" he asked, realizing there was little more than he could say *decently*. He visibly panted, fought not to pursue her.

"Sure," she whispered, opening the door for herself.

She was still in a daze, trying to wrap her mind around what had just happened. Plus, there was a child here. She had to go. Even though she wanted to stay and see what else Mitch could do well, she simply had to leave.

Chapter Five

It was a rainy Sunday morning and Elaine was due back at any moment. Relaxing in front of the television, Mitch and Zach watched a soccer game while eating leftovers from LaToya's huge meal on Friday.

Buckets of water splashed against the window and wind beat against the shutters. But the tranquil calmness inside made both of them forget about the weather. Today, they were happy.

It had been a long time since the house had been spotless for his visitation with his son. Mitch appreciated the fact that they could dwell in the large space without falling over boxes and papers. He watched his son relaxed and enjoying their time together and felt a sense of ease that he had not felt since Elaine left.

Resting his head back on the couch, he closed his eyes and thought involuntarily of LaToya's warm mouth again. He could feel her hot breath on his skin and the taste of her marvelous, velvety tongue. The hair began to rise on his arm and goose bumps formed. *He had kissed LaToya.* The thought made him lick his lips, trying to recall every sensation again, but nothing would do. He needed the real thing.

Glancing over at his cell phone, he grabbed it up and went into the other room. The phone dialed and rang for only a minute, then LaToya answered. Her voice was sweet and calming.

"Hello," she said smiling.

"LaToya," Mitch swallowed hard. "What are you doing?"

"Sitting in my library reading."

"You have a library?" He looked in the media room at the large television mounted on the wall and suddenly felt inferior.

"I guess you could call it that. It's mine. So, that's what I call it."

"Do you have some huge mansion on a hill?" he joked.

LaToya laughed. "My house is smaller than one part of your downstairs."

"But I bet it's beautiful."

LaToya looked around the room and shook her head. "I think so."

Mitch took a deep breath and lowered his voice. "I'd like to see it."

There was silence on the line.

"Your library, I mean," he said, running his hand through is hair.

"I know what you meant," she said softly. "I'm trying to decide if that's a good idea or not."

"You've seen my place. Why shouldn't I see yours?"

"Because it's unprofessional, and I'm attempting really hard to keep your business, Mitch O'Keefe."

Mitch smiled. *So, it was hard for her too.* "I want to see you again, and I don't want to wait.

Can I come over to see your *library* and talk to you?"

"Aren't you babysitting?"

"Well, it's not really babysitting. He's my kid." He scratched his head again and looked in the room at his son still watching the game. "Plus, he'll be gone in just a bit. Then, I'll be here alone, and I don't have anything to do today. And even if I did..."

"Mitch, you're rambling."

"I know. Can you help me out? Say yes."

There was silence on the phone.

"Yes." She finally gave in to his pleas. "I'll text you my address. What time?"

"As soon as Elaine arrives."

"About what time will that be?"

"Three."

"Okay. I'll see you at four," she answered

"3:30," he replied. "And not a minute later."

She giggled. "Fine. 3:30 it is."

***

Usually when Elaine arrived to Mitch's house, there was always a heated argument laced with hurtful words, pleas and confusion. She braced herself for the torture of a broken marriage as she rang the doorbell. *What would he have to say today?* she thought.

Nervously, she looked back at her fiancé, who was sitting in the car looking out the window at her, awaiting the drama and ready to attack. His car sat idly with the lights on her while the windshield wipers made swift evolutions back and forth on the glass as she stood in under her large pink umbrella in the downpour of rain.

Annoyed, she rang the doorbell again, taking out her frustration on the small, glowing button. After a large crack of thunder behind her made her nearly jump out of her shoes, the door quickly swung open and smells of food, bleach and cinnamon potpourri met her. She was speechless. For the first time since *the disaster*, she caught a glimpse of the Mitch she knew many years ago.

Behind him, was a glow of candles and dim lights. Around him was a glow of happiness. With a bright, telling smile on his perfectly shaped lips, Mitch called for Zach to get his bags because his mother, *not Elaine*, had arrived to pick him up. Hands out of his pockets and his wedding ring off, he invited her in.

"Hi Elaine," he said warmly. "How was your trip? Please come in. It's raining."

Elaine was speechless. Clutching her purse, she looked back at Felix and then stepped very carefully inside out of the rain into the foyer.

This time she looked around the house and noticed that it was immaculate. She had missed that fact a few days before, so taken by the dark, black woman, who claimed to be his *cleaning friend*.

"Is he already ready for us?" Elaine asked, surprised that Mitch had gotten him dressed and packed on time for once.

"Yes," he said, looking down the foyer. "Zach, hurry, man."

Elaine stood stupefied. "Are you alright?" she asked. "You look different."

Mitch turned to her and shook his head. "I'm fine...perfect." His Irish accent was thick and sexy. His baritone was only made sexier by the low, growl of his voice and the taut muscles that ran up his neck as he spoke.

Oh my God, he's sexy again, she thought as she noticed also that he had started to work out again. Swallowing hard at his sudden appeal, the smell of his cologne, his overall confidence, she stumbled over her words. "Good. I mean, I'm glad that you're well," she said baffled. She wiped her wet bangs from her face.

He blinked. His face was unreadable.

"LaToya was very nice by the way." Her woman's intuition kicked in as she searched her mind for possibilities of his transformation. The only thing different in his life was *that woman*.

Mitch nodded by didn't reply. Instead, he bent down to one knee as his son came down the corridor and grabbed him.

"Alright, buddy, see you next weekend." He kissed Zach's cheek. "I love you so very, very much."

"Love you too, Dad. I had fun with you. Tell LaToya I said bye." He kissed his father and pulled his luggage out in the rain to the Mercedes waiting for him. On cue, Felix jumped out of the car and popped the trunk open to load the boy.

Mitch watched for a minute and then snapped out of his daze.

"Is she still here?" Elaine asked.

"Is *who* still here," Mitch asked, looking at his watch. 2:53.

"LaToya, *your cleaning lady*. He said to tell her *goodbye*. Is she still here? I'd like to tell her thank you also." She looked back into the house, wanting badly to break free of his invisible barriers to see who lurked upstairs in his bedroom. Jealousy began to pinch at her heart. Suddenly, she could remember how skilled her husband use to be in bed and it killed her to think another woman might know the same pleasure.

Mitch narrowed his mossy green eyes on his ex-wife and pulled his keys out of his pocket. "Let me help you to the car," he said, escorting her out of the door. He closed the door behind him and checked it. "I'm sorry I kept you waiting so long in the rain. You're drenched."

His simple acknowledgement of her made her heart skip a beat. She walked right beside him, instep with his every moment for the first time in many years. Suddenly, it felt good to be beside him, good to know him. She took in a deep breath of his cologne and clenched her jaw. *Damn you, Mitch O'Keefe*, she thought as heat started to boil from her core.

As he walked her out, Mitch nodded at Felix for the first time ever. Elaine looked over again dumbfounded.

"Thanks for bringing my son over," he said, looking down at her as the rainwater hit his lips and the dimple in his chin. His eyes gleamed with a happiness that she could not understand.

"You're welcome," she whispered.

Mitch stopped midway between their car and his front door, refusing to go any further with her. As she walked hesitantly back to the man that she had left him for, she looked back at her ex-husband. The water seemed to hit him just right. It made him more beautiful, and painfully, it washed away the hold she had on him for so many years. Flashes of their life together passed through her mind. Their wedding. Her son's christening. Their many happy days. It seemed to all wash away.

He stood bulging with rippling muscles under a wet, gray t-shirt clinging to his body around his taut biceps lined with veins, his thick neck, and his carved abs. The rain soaked his pants, and made them stick to his wide, muscular legs chiseled like stone from many years of playing soccer. His curly, tousled hair stuck around his tanned face and brought out his mossy green eyes and his sexy freckles sprinkled over his perfect nose and rose-dusted lips. He was a picture of perfection. Suddenly, she could see that and it was painful to watch.

She got in the passenger seat and looked out at him, standing in the rain watching his family leave him. Only this time, he didn't seem to want her to stay. And this time, she didn't want to go.

Nearly in slow motion, she watched him. Hitting the button on his key chain, the garage door opened to Mitch's Toyota Tundra, and he quickly ran inside to it away from her and probably *to* LaToya.

She wiped the tear away and tried to smile at Felix, but he watched her as closely as she watched Mitch. Without saying a word, he backed up out of the driveway.

Before they could get down the street from his home, Mitch had already passed them in the splashing water, headed towards Phoenix in his truck. And he never looked back.

***

LaToya rushed about the house quickly, spraying sprays and scents on her body and on the furniture. The house was cleaned with not even a speckle of dirt, but she still had to arrange and rearrange considering a man had never been to her home before for the purpose of seeing her *library* or whatever.

Changing clothes in her bathroom, she slipped on a pair of jeans, thinking the restriction of such a garment would surely make her safer from his touch. She also piled on a tank-top, then a v-neck t-shirt just to make sure enough layers were there to remind her before she was naked of what she was doing.

Pulling her braids up in a wispy ponytail, she checked her makeup in the mirror and caught a glimpse of the weight scale in its reflection. She paused and looked over at it. It eyed her, and she eyed it back. There was a mental war going on between them, wondering if the numbers that little scale revealed would be the thing to keep her from the man who would be ringing her doorbell at any moment.

And just then, the doorbell rang.

She walked passed it, avoiding stepping too close, and darted to the front door.

The rain had just released another downpour. The winds had picked up, and Mitch was drenched, but he stood smiling as if the sun was shining directly on him. As soon as his foot hit the threshold of her home, he grabbed her in his embrace. Unable to wait, driven mad by the drive over from his place, he wrapped his wet arms around her and held her close. She held him back like she had not seen him in years. Their eyes met only seconds before their lips intertwined in a hot, mesmerizing kiss. Her knees became weak at the taste of his minty tongue swirling through her needy mouth. With each kiss, he drove himself deeper down into her heart, reaching finally to the core of her. The rain continued to rip through the door and drench them both, but they ignored it and continued to kiss.

LaToya managed in her divine insanity to flick her wrist hard enough to close the door while he consumed her, but she nearly lost consciousness after it shut. Kissing him back with the same heated passion that he provided, they found their way to the couch in her living room where he hovered over her, fists planted firmly into her leather sofa and muscles tense with wanton desire. He disappeared in the softness of her lips again, tasting the fleshy sweetness that caused his burn to boil.

She could feel all nine inches of him as he rocked his hips forward. Her skin instantly lit on fire with sensations that had been so long forgotten she didn't know that they were still real. Widening her legs, she felt him lower himself in between her. Hot blood rushed up into his tense legs and through his throbbing penis. He planted himself just atop her aching sex, grinding against the softness of her body.

His thighs trembled as he thought about what he wanted, but instead, he continued to kiss her. Leaning over with one elbow beside her, he let his right hand relax to run over her large breasts. Unable to help himself, he pinched her pebbled nipple.

LaToya let out a gasp of both pain and pleasure. Every nerve ending in her body was firing all at once. Her eyes opened and she gazed up into the green abyss of his eyes. *I have to stop this now or I'll never stop it*, she thought to herself.

Reluctantly, LaToya finally hampered her raw emotion and tapped at his rock-solid chest for him to pull back. He did so obediently panting at her feet like a good canine. She ran her hand through his tousled hair and leaned down to place her forehead on his. *I can't believe you're here*, she thought to herself.

"Your library is fabulous, by the way," he said smiling.

She wiped the rainwater from his freckled nose.

"Thank you," she replied, "but this is my living room. My library is down the hall." Coming out of her heated state, she realized that they were now soaking wet.

Mitch looked around the room and nodded. "Well, this room is nice too."

***

The rain beat down on the rooftop while Mitch and LaToya sat in her second bedroom, *turned into a library*, and drank mimosas while she showed him her record collection. They had been holed up for hours eating, laughing and kissing.

Mitch thumbed through to her records, given to her by her mother, and ate his seventh finger sandwich.

"So, your mother gave you all these records?" he asked, sucking his teeth.

"Yep," LaToya said, proudly looking at her collection of over 500 records. "There in perfect condition, too. I listen to them on her record player when I read. Plus, it's better than the music they play on the radio these days. It's relaxing. "

"This entire place is relaxing. I could stay in here forever. It's so warm and cozy like a home should be," he said, lying back on the pillow. "You must like living alone. It's so tranquil." He tapped his bare feet on the carpet, wiggling his toes happily.

"It has its perks." She put down her glass. "And it has its draw backs. Everyone wants someone. I'm no different in that I suppose."

He turned to look at her. "No, you're not different in that. I want the same thing. I'm at the age where I need someone to love and someone to love me. That's where I messed up the first time with Elaine. I gave her the world, but I never noticed that she didn't give anything in return."

She quickly changed the subject, seeing that just the thought of her still pained him. "So, you've been in the states for twenty years. You were married for eleven. You have one kid. And you're close to making partner." She smiled. "You've accomplished a lot in a short period of time, but how old are you?"

"Forty," he smiled. "Don't I look it?"

"You don't look a day over 30."

"Well, thank you for the gracious compliment. But I don't feel like 30. As my son gets older, I feel older. Watching him grow up is the greatest treasure in the world, but with every inch and every pound he gains, I also gain a wrinkle, a gray hair. It puts my mortality into perspective." He shoved the rest of the sandwich in his mouth with his index finger.

"I want kids someday. I want the house filled with construction paper and homework and class projects and report cards." She grinned. "You're so lucky to have Zach. He's amazing."

"A woman like you could have all of that and more. I mean, I'm sure that you'd be a great mom. You cook; you clean. You make everyone feel like they're special. Zach fell in love with you in just one day, and trust me when I say that he's guarded. I could just imagine what your own kids would think of you."

Sitting up, he caught LaToya looking at his bare chest. She had taken his shirt off and put it in the dryer hours ago.

"Want your shirt back?" she asked softly. She bit her lip and looked away.

He looked down at his body and looked back up at her. "Would you like to join me...take off your shirt?"

LaToya shook her head. "No. I wouldn't." She blushed.

"Why not?"

She couldn't bring herself to say that she was fat. *Why couldn't he just see it?* Rolling her eyes, she tried to lie. "I don't like taking my shirt off."

Mitch bit his bottom lip. *He'd take it off for her if she'd let him.* Crawling on his knees across the room towards her, he snaked up to her body, in between her legs and moved her braids out of her face.

Studying her features, he dipped in to kiss her lips again, stroking his tongue along the roof of her perfect mouth, slowly committing her fruity taste to memory. She tasted like heaven. Her mewling sounds of pleasure sounded like hypnotic tunes of ecstasy. He literally could kiss her for days on end. The flesh on flesh made him forget that the outside world existed. She dipped her head back and allowed him to trail sensual, sweet kisses down her neck.

Trailing his finger over her bottom lip, he whispered in a husky voice. "Let me see what you look like, LaToya. I'm dying to know." A promise of pleasure colored his face. His clever grin made her heart skip a beat. "For everything that you show me, I'll show you mine in return," he bargained.

LaToya could feel his hot breath on her skin setting it on fire again and smell his cologne making her drunk with blind desire. She looked into his eyes and marveled at how sincere he seemed. Shaking her head, she pulled away.

"Mitch, we have to slow down." Patting him, she stood up and smoothed out her clothes.

He looked up at her. "Slow down? Why? Did I do something?"

"No. Why do you always think that you've done something wrong?" She clenched her jaw. "Look, before you even jump to conclusions, I'm not trying to play hard to get here. I want us to slow down before something happens. I don't know about you, but I haven't been with anyone in some years. I imagine by now, I could have been, but I don't want to get hurt again."

"Well, I don't want to get hurt either." He sat on his behind. With his knees cocked up, he rested his elbows on his thighs. "And I don't want to hurt you, LaToya. If you think that I'm some kind of playboy - ". He nervously ran his hand through his hair and looked up at her.

"I don't," she cut him off. "I would have never invited you here, if I thought that you were any-thing but sincere."

"Then what is it? It has to be something. We're both adults. We're both single. We're both at-tracted to one another. I can't imagine that there is any more reason not to continue forward."

"I don't want to be the rebound girl that you bided your time away with until something better came along." Licking her dry lips, she pulled at her shirt, uncomfortable with his confused stare. "You at least have your son. You have...so much. It would be easy for you to get over moving too fast with me. But I wouldn't be able to get over it that easy. I need to slow down for me."

He understood, but he wouldn't back down. "I don't want to *use* you like that. Trust me, it's been done to me, and it's no way to treat a person. I like you. I want to spend time with you. I want to get to know you outside of our working relationship." He shrugged his muscular shoulders. "But I won't pressure you. It would devastate me if I ever hurt you."

His words were sobering. A man had not been so honest about his feelings for her in a very long time. She was humbled by his willingness. "Thank you," she said softly. "Just give me a little time before we move to ripping each other's clothes off. You know. Let's work into this and make sure that we're making the right decisions. If it's going to work, it's going to work. Right?"

He stood up and walked over to her. Wrapping his arms around her, he kissed the top of her head and sighed. "Fair enough. I'm willing to work for it, *but* if you don't want me to continue to think about ripping things off of you, I'd suggest you give me back my clothing and let me take you to dinner. Because, I'm starving for something, and I rather like the idea of having you as my main entrée."

They both laughed.

Chapter Six

LaToya rushed quickly through her other houses to get to Mitch's place. She had even re-arranged her schedule over the last couple of weeks to ensure that his stop was the last of the day.

Things between them had been slow but enjoyable. Her *no-sex* rule was driving him mad, but he continued to respect her wishes, while still getting to know her better each and every day. They talked about everything from politics to first loves. He was always open and candid and often extremely insightful. She enjoyed his company immensely and it had truly been the first time in her life that she was developing a friendship with someone as well as a stable foundation for a relationship.

Today, she cleaned the house perfectly, as normal, and then retired to the kitchen to fix them dinner. It was strange to be his girlfriend and *cleaning lady*. Often, she would hurry to clean their dishes after a meal just to make cleaning up the next day easier on herself.

Mitch laughed at how hard she tried and often went the extra mile to clean himself, unlike before.

She had turned on the skillet and was cutting up onions when she heard his feet on the tile in the hallway. With a smile on her lips, she kept her back to him as she cooked, just so he could walk up behind her and kiss her neck.

He did not disappoint.

She felt his soft lips against her skin and his hands on her arms. He bent to her ear and whispered. "I have the most exciting news." His voice made her eyes flutter.

She turned and looked up at him. "What?"

"I got a promotion today." He sauntered over to the cabinet and pulled out two wine glasses. "Well, it's a little more than a promotion, really." Opening a bottle of wine, he poured them both a glass and then passed it to her. "I made partner." He grinned.

LaToya cracked a wide smile. "That's wonderful."

He sipped a little wine and leaned on the counter. "Isn't it?" He shook his head. "I still can't believe it myself. They told me today. We make it official at the end of next week. There will be an announcement at the Hadley dinner."

"The Hadley dinner?" she asked confused.

"It's this big deal. I was trying to figure out a way to get out of going until today." He cocked his brow at her and took another drink. "Speaking of which, what are you doing on next Friday night?"

"The Hadley dinner, I guess." She raised her glass to him and grinned. "I'm so proud of you."

"Thanks," he said as he grabbed his cell. "I have to call Zach and tell him. He'll be so happy. I've been wearing his ear out about it for months now. Why don't you finish up here, and I'll get settled and be right down for dinner." Kissing her on the forehead, he winked and walked away.

***

The weekend came quickly, and on Sunday, LaToya and her friends decided to get together at Angela's loft for drinks at dusk. This was the first weekend since Mitch and she had been dating that they were not together.

She tried hard to focus on the women and not send texts revealing her ultimate boredom with them. Also, she had not shared with them yet that she was seeing him. There were many reasons for it, but mostly, she just wanted to see if their relationship was going to work first. So far, every indication said that it would. And she really hoped that it would. Her life had not been so easy in a very long time. She glowed in the morning now and went to bed every night feeling like she had just found the garden of Eden.

LaToya walked around Angela's swank, two-bedroom penthouse admiring how well she had done for herself. She was a successful CPA – one of the best-known women professionals in the city. On her walls were many accolades from different associations, distinguished degrees, articles written about her and awe striking pictures for all to see. There were even photos of all the famous people that she had met during her career and even dated. *Angela had it all.* And LaToya liked her friend, because even though she was incredibly charismatic and successful, she was down to earth and loving.

Angela was the type to already be the center of attention at an event and still introduce whom many called her *ugly girlfriend*. LaToya hated the title she had picked up, but recently, she didn't feel like that woman anymore. And the fact that she kept her love a secret made her feel all the more elusive.

Then there was Deana. Deana was a petite black woman with short, curly hair and big brown eyes who never had a problem getting a man, even when he wasn't the right one.

But LaToya was the one woman at an event who hardly ever went home with a number, and normally even if she did get a guy's number, she never called, because she knew in his book, she wasn't the first choice, just the only choice who wasn't already taken. And while to many she was the ugly girlfriend, she wasn't desperate. So, she wasn't about to pick a man who thought she was.

The music playing was suddenly turned down low drawing her attention from the picture of Angela with a well-known actor to the current event. "Alright, we've had dinner. We're having drinks," Angela said, sitting down in the middle of her white Armani sofa and putting her feet up. "Now, it's time to dish, ladies. What has been going on with you?"

Deana chimed in first. During the last two weeks, she had stopped seeing her married man and had decided to give an old love interest one more chance to get it right. No one was surprised by Deana. She dated at a reckless rate and hardly ever looked for love. As a rep for a local record label, she spent most of her time looking for the *next big thing* and equated everything in life to the same standard.

"Stony is back in town," Deana explained. "It seems like this time, it might be a good relationship. Now, that he's finally financially stable," she continued, "he can start to really focus."

"But can you?" Angela asked her like a therapist.

"I...think so," she smiled. "I'll try. You can't ask anymore than that of me. Besides, he lost a lot of weight and looks really good. I think 40 is the new 30 for him."

Angela quickly moved the conversation to herself. "Well, Byron and I are really getting serious. And I just feel bad for him. He wasn't chosen as partner. Mitch was. Everyone knows that it's because he's white. I mean, Byron works harder, smarter and the clients love him. Plus, he's been there longer, but he's not the right shade. He's really thinking about quitting. Do you know that Mitch works from home most of the time? All the partners were *so* sorry about his breakup with his wife. Now, if he had been a brother, they would have told him to suck it up and be to work on time."

Both Angela and Deana looked over at LaToya. She listened attentively with a scowl on her face. She didn't even realize that she was betraying her hidden relationship. It was obvious to everyone that the mere mention of him in a negative light frustrated her.

"So have you heard anything, LaToya?" Angela asked as she tilted her head and batted her eyelashes.

LaToya put down her glass and smirked. "You could have just asked," she said, hitting IGNORE on her phone as Mitch called.

"Well, I *am* asking," Angela said softly. "I'm concerned about Byron and you know that this isn't right." Her voice changed as she saw LaToya's eyebrows spike.

"I don't know about it not being right. Mitch works really hard," LaToya defended. "And while sometimes, he works from home, he puts in a lot of time." She felt terribly uncomfortable about explaining his business to them, but she tried hard to be sensible considering these were her friends. "The only people who can decide if he's really qualified to be a partner in the firm or not are the partners, not us."

Angela rolled her eyes. "You can't be serious. We're all three black women in here. We know what types of prejudice bigots are out there."

"I'm not oblivious to the world, Angela."

"But you defend a man who clearly doesn't deserve this promotion, because why?" She shrugged her shoulders. "Are you seeing him or something?"

LaToya walked over to the couch and sat down. "Yes, as a matter of fact, I am. But that has nothing to do with my opinion of this situation."

Deana raised her brows. "Okay, touchy, touchy. Let's change the subject."

"Let's *not* change the subject." Angela waved a finger in the air in protest. "LaToya, how can you say that a *brother* who is more qualified, has more seniority and is a product of Phoenix, should not make partner before a guy like Mitch?"

"And what kind of guy is Mitch, Angela?" LaToya piped up.

"Just another white boy who could fit in better at the golf course."

"You don't know what you're talking about," LaToya said angrily. "Mitch works all day, not just at the firm. He works all night long, too. He graduated from Harvard with honors. He's worked on sites all over the world, and regardless of his race, he's an asset."

"And Byron's not?"

"I don't know. I don't know anything about Bryon except that he has more black slacks than any man I've ever cleaned for, and he could use a new pool boy."

Deana laughed.

Angela rolled her eyes. "I think your past relationship has jaded you against black men. So, now because you've been rejected so much by them, you would tend to side with the other side. How else could you sit here and defend Mitch over Byron?"

"I'm not defending as much as I am saying that we cannot make that call as simply their girlfriends. Neither one of us has been in a relationship with either one of those men long enough to know. We're on the outside looking in."

"It doesn't take a rocket scientist to see that this is the same *good ole boy* network working at its finest to keep good black men out of the jobs that they clearly deserve."

"Angela, that may very well be so, but I don't know for sure. And because I don't know, and because I'm in a relationship with him, I'm simply saying that from my point of view, his qualifications make him a viable candidate for the position as well."

"Well, let me ask you this then. Once he gets this promotion, do you think that he's going to show up with you on his arm? I mean, you are his cleaning lady. Do you think that he's going to tell that story over dinner with his senior partners? Do you think he's going to pass your card to a client and suggest that they try his girlfriend's cleaning service? Do you think that he'll even present you to his friends and his *good ole boy* network? I can answer all those questions for you, LaToya. Hell no. He is not. And while you're sitting here taking up for him, no one will ever even know that he had a fling with the maid. That's some old southern, plantation shit, okay. White men have always had a little black thing that they messed off with and no one knew. You two ain't doing nothing new under the sun."

LaToya shook her head in disgust. "You don't have a clue what he's about."

"Neither do you. Do you think that just because he's screwing you that suddenly he's an honorary black man? Don't be so blind. Most importantly sister, don't be a sellout."

"Don't you ever accuse me on the sly of being an Uncle Tom just because I don't agree with you. Me of all people," LaToya hit her chest. "The woman who is often too black for black men or too fat for the prime pick of black men. I will never sit in front of a woman like you, some Beyonce look-alike, and try to defend my position, because it's women like me who know what it truly feels like to be denied and rejected by both races. I feel the way that I feel about Mitch's promotion because I know the man. And for your information, not that it is any of your business, I'm not *screwing* him. We happen to be building a relationship, something that's about more than just being a notch on his belt. And while you're sitting here trying to read me my rights, what makes you think that he's going to march your ass down the aisle and put a ring on your finger or for that matter just present you at his next dinner? You know because you know him, just like I know Mitch. And I don't approve of you trying to belittle me or belittle my relationship just because a promotion didn't work out for your boyfriend." LaToya snapped. "You know what...I'm out of here," she said, grabbing her purse. "You call me when you have more respect and not for my boyfriend but for me."

***

The next morning, on schedule, LaToya arrived at Bryon's home to clean his house at nine. With her cleaning baskets in hand, she turned off his alarm and headed to the kitchen, where he normally left any important notes.

His home was much cleaner than normal. *Yeah for me*, she thought. A sense of happiness came over her, knowing she could finish much sooner today.

Placing her baskets carefully on his kitchen counter, she noticed an envelope waiting for her with her name elegantly written on the front. She opened it quickly, tearing the edges of the sealed paper and pulling out a small piece of stationary. Reading it quietly, she waded up the paper after she was finished and threw it in the garbage.

Grabbing her baskets, she headed back out of the house and decided to go to Mitch's place.

***

LaToya unlocked Mitch's front door and came inside without knocking. She didn't need to do that anymore. He had told her that about a hundred times now. Every time that she announced herself, he would admonish her. *Who else would be here if not me*? he would ask. *Just make yourself comfortable,* he would say. *My home is your home,* he would remind.   Setting down her baskets, she was surprised to see the alarm was off.

Maybe I'll feel better if I just make me something to eat, she thought. Her new diet was killing her, and although she had managed to lose five pounds, she still had an appetite like a lion.

As she walked down the corridor to the kitchen, she halted when she heard two voices. Stopping in her tracks, she pushed against the side of the wall and listened, slowing even her breathing to hear them clearer.

"Why now, Elaine?" Mitch asked frustrated. His heavy accent was thick with confusion and strained with annoyance.

"Why not now? What would happen if I waited until it was too late?"

"And what makes you think that it's not already too late for Christ's sake! We're divorced. We've ripped our son's heart out and torn it to pieces. Now, you want to come back? Do I have the word *idiot* written on my face? Is that what you take me for? Just because I try hard to be civil does not mean that I'm some push over."

"I've always loved you, Mitchell," she begged. "You have to know that."

"And I always loved you, Elaine, but it didn't stop you from fucking my son's pediatrician! It didn't stop you from getting pregnant by him. It definitely didn't stop you from ruining our family. Now, you want to come back? I'm in complete disbelief. I am. I can't believe my ears."

LaToya held her heart. She couldn't believe her ears either. In her mind, she had always prepared for competition outside of the home, but she didn't know if she even had the ammunition to handle his ex-wife. They had so much history together. *Hell, they had a child together.*

"But we could make it work," Elaine pleaded softly. She walked up to him and held his face in her manicured, delicate hands. Her stiletto heels clinked against the tile and her gold bangles rattled as she moved into him. Melting into his body, she leaned in to kiss his lips, but he quickly moved away. "I know that you still love me," she whispered.

Grabbing her hands, Mitch shook his head. "Stop it, Elaine." He swallowed hard.

"Why?"

Mitch smacked his lips, tired with the entire conversation. "I'm in love with someone else that's why."

"What?" Elaine looked up at him confused. She searched his face. "The cleaning lady? I thought that you were just kidding to make me jealous. You actually love that fat bitch?" Her voice raised.

Mitch pushed her away. "You have no right to say those types of things about her. She's beautiful and she's smart and she's worth a hell of a lot more than you."

"Mitchell, she's just looking for a payday," Elaine said facetiously.

"And you aren't. It's funny that you didn't want a damned thing to do with me until you heard about me making partner."

There was silence.

She finally looked up from the ground. "That's not true. I wanted you when I saw you here the other day. It was just something about you that made me realize how foolish I've been."

Mitch listened carefully, never taking his eyes off of her.

"The promotion just made me realize how hard we worked to get you to this point. And the more I thought about it, the more I realized that I had made a mistake," she explained.

Mitch leaned against the counter and sighed. His muscular chest caved in under his weight. "You made a mistake? Mistakes come in the form of forgetting to pay a bill or pick up the dry cleaning or even toying with the idea of leaving. What you did was a little more than a mistake, dear. It would be better placed under the classification of a catastrophic disaster. And that promotion was always your dream, not mine," Mitch said angrily.

He stood up. "I was happy to get it, but you were the one who pushed me. You wanted me to leave New York and come here. You wanted me to take on the hard projects to make partner. And then when I didn't get it first off when I got here, you flew the coop and left me for the failure I was. Then you tried to make it be my fault. You told me that because I was never home, you had fallen in *Felix's* arms. But it was you who sent me out to get the job done. I was damned if I did, damned if I did not." He wiped the hot tears from his face. "Now you criticize the woman who literally helped me clean my life back up after you left me here to rot, because I wasn't good enough." He smirked. "You're a fucking bitch, Elaine. You're the ugly one."

Enraged, Elaine reached back and slapped his face. Her gold bracelets jingled as her sweaty hand made contact with his jaw. "You really are a world class loser, Mitchell. You always will be."

"That's me. Your everyday, average, world-class, loser. Take care of the kids. Take care of the ex-wife. Take care of it all and get nothing." He hit the table and made her jump, "Nothing in response except a slap in the face. I have given you every-thing and you gave me nothing." His face red-dened. "Get out of my house. Go home to your *Felix* and play doctor."

LaToya wiped the tears from her eyes as their conversation ended. That was certainly more than she had anticipated on hearing, but she had to know if he cared for her the way that she cared for him. Now certain of that fact, she turned to walk away, to give him the privacy he needed, but he heard her footsteps and stepped into the hallway.

"LaToya?" he said shocked. His voice echoed down the empty hall. "How long have you been here?"

LaToya took a long, deep breath and then turned around. She had tears on her cheeks run-ning plentifully down her neck. "Long enough," she said, trying to smile. "I promise that I didn't mean to pry. Really, I didn't. It's just been a long day. I just sort of found myself here." She tried to dry her eyes as she explained.

"Well, this is where you belong," he said lovingly.

Walking to her, he grabbed her in his arms and held her close. She hugged him back, happy to be in his embrace. Tears ran down her cheek onto his white polo, and she felt his warms lips on the side of her face. She could even smell Elaine's perfume as she dashed past both of them and slammed the door on her way out.

Chapter Seven

LaToya called in her staff to clean the rest of her houses that night. In the state that both she and Mitch were in, they both really just needed to be together. As usual, she cooked dinner for them, and they sat at the kitchen table talking.

"I think I just had a break through," Mitch said proudly. "Before you, I would have never been able to tell that woman how I really felt. It was liberating."

LaToya smiled. "Before you, I would have never felt more important than Angela." She frowned then. "It only occurred to me after Byron fired me that maybe the only reason that she was so kind to me is because she never felt that I was on her level. Then at the slightest hint of me having more than her, she turned on me." She shook her head. "And had her boyfriend fire me."

"Now that was just plain stupid on his part." He smiled. "I could have him fired, you know."

"Don't," she warned. "I'm already a sell out."

"What?" He looked up from his dinner. He had been in states long enough to know what that was.

"There was a huge argument about you and Byron at Angela's house last night. She thinks that you only got the promotion, because you're white."

"Oh. I suppose that it could easily be misperceived here in this country." He looked down at his dinner. "And you had to take up for me, did you?"

"Yeah," she said sighing. "I know how hard you work."

"Well, I'm very sorry that I came between you and your good friend."

LaToya smiled at him. "You didn't do anything wrong. I'm still just as proud of you today as I was before she told me about Byron."

"That's the thing, LaToya. I don't... I don't want to work this hard for the rest of my life. I want to live, you know. I want to be there for Zach and spend more time enjoying my real life. Do you know that this house is paid for? My car is paid for." He sighed again. "I work my ass off for stuff, but at the end of the day I was just not happy. Somewhere along the lines, I lost what I was doing all of this for. And society says that you have to keep going."

"Society is bullshit," she said quickly. "You decide your own destiny. If you don't want this, why do you do it?"

"I don't know," he half way laughed. "I've been asking myself that a lot lately. I felt the most fulfilled doing non-profit work. The buildings that we designed for worthy causes always made me feel...I don't know...more centered. I'm going to work this partnership and milk it for all it's worth, then I'm going to leave and start my own firm where I take on good causes like building hospitals in third-world countries." He stabbed his steak and then paused. "Why do you clean people's houses?"

"I'm a neat freak. I can't help myself," she laughed. "It's true. I actually enjoy organizing people's lives." She looked down at her plate. "And I guess I'm like you, because I save every penny. I plan to retire early and enjoy my life, too. And I shouldn't have given a damn about one lousy account today, and normally I wouldn't have, but it was because of Angela that it hurt."

"Trust me, sister. I know a thing or two about hurt," he reassured.

"I know," LaToya said, looking up at him. "But it's not your fault. What she did to you was horrible and inconsiderate." She let the tears fall down her face again, "And I know that that kind of pain doesn't go away quickly, but one day it will. Trust me. And you can sit across the table from a guy having dinner and see that the best of your years really aren't behind you. And that there are good men out there who mean what they say and do what they say."

Mitch was speechless. He cracked a grin finally. "I hope it's not a guy that makes me feel like that, LaToya."

They both laughed.

LaToya quickly wiped her face. "Well, you are sort of...sweet," she said looking down.

"Well, you are, too."

Mitch set down his fork, moved his napkin off his lap and stood up. LaToya looked up at him. He walked around the table to her and kneeled at her chair. "We've been doing this no sex relationship for a while, and I totally respect what you're doing, but tonight made me realize that I'm ready to take it to the next level with you, if you're ready." His words were soft, barely above a whisper. They were as intimate as the action he was suggesting. "Because I am sitting across from the woman who I know is enhancing every part of my life except one."

Her lips parted and she pushed the words out. "I don't know if I'll ever be ready. I haven't had sex in so long, I'm not sure that I remember how to." Her clever remark was lost on him.

He smirked. "I can show you. It's very much like riding a bike, love."

LaToya stopped smiling. "I want to make love to you, Mitch. But what if it completely ruins what we have right now?"

"How can it?"

"Sex makes things weird. You no longer open up; you become secretive."

"Who is *you*? *I* don't do that. *I* become more open with a woman after sex." He looked her in her eyes. "If you're afraid, I understand. But I want you to take that leap with me anyway. Trust me."

"Leap?"

"Yes, leap?" He smiled. "Right of the cliff."

LaToya took a deep breath and put down her napkin. Standing up, she took his hand and followed him quietly out of the kitchen.

***

LaToya had cleaned Mitch's room a hundred times, but she had never once been in it for any other reason. It looked different now that she was a guest. The king-sized bed looked larger, warmer and more inviting under the soft lights.

Candles that she had lit earlier to freshen the room were now used to provide seductive lighting under the busy fan that made violent revolutions above them.

Mitch had a languid grin on his face as he stood in front of her, bent into the curve of her voluptuous body and looking into her deep brown eyes. He tried to read them for instruction as he rubbed her shoulders. It had been decided by him as soon as she agreed to make love that he would take this night as slow as she needed.

Zingers of wild, erotic sensations ran rapidly through her anxious body.

"Are you on the pill?" he asked, eyebrows spiking.

"No." She shook her head.

"Well, I have protection." He dipped his head to her lightly kissed her lips.

"I'm scared, Mitch," she whispered on his lips.

"Me too," he assured. "But I love you, LaToya."

She looked up into his simmering, green eyes flashing with hope and sincerity and suddenly felt at ease. Those three words made all the difference.

"I love you, too," she said, smiling as she confessed her love. Her heart instantly exploded.

Looking down at her shirt, she pulled it slowly off, revealing the shape that she had so desperately tried to hide for so long.

Mitch felt his breath catch in his throat. He tried not to show his hidden excitement. Even the smallest reveal heightened his already thrilled senses. Her decadent, soft chocolate skin was a beautiful, uninterrupted shade of deep mahogany that reminded him of the purest silk. Her large breasts were cupped together in a black bra shaped into a perfect heart. He looked at the crease that separated them, licking his lips with anticipation of taste.

Her long torso was shapely and full. Marveling at seeing a plus size woman for the first time nearly naked, he was completely fascinated by the un-marked, unstressed perfect darkness before him like a faultless night.

Crossing her arms across her body, she tried to hide herself, but he quickly pulled them away and made her show herself. Stepping into her, he felt her breast graze his chest. It was then that he realized that he was fully dressed.

Remembering his bedroom manners, he took off his shirt, snatching it from his body quickly to reveal a tanned, muscular build that defied his profession. He broad shoulders and thick muscles dwarfed her. LaToya noticed a sweet little beauty mole on his left oblique muscle. It looked delectable.

He placed her quivering hand on his chest in hopes that she would allow him the same offering. She caressed his muscles, fascinated by his perfectly carved body.

His hands softly wrapped around her, accelerating their heat as he plucked her bra straps. The garment fell to the floor between them and caused an ache in his groin. How he loved perfect breasts. LaToya's breasts were large, full and ripe with sensual chocolate bits aroused at the tip.

He kneeled down to taste them, wrapping his wet mouth around her areola and suckling at her nipples slowly. He moaned hungrily as he tasted her, putting his hands around the full orbs for a better grip. Every time that he pulled away to look at her, the wind from the ceiling fan tickled her senses. She gasped in the silence of the room, creaming for him involuntarily between her hot thighs as she watched him taste her. It was so intoxicating to watch as he moved and tasted her with utter care.

LaToya didn't realize that her mouth was open. The seduction of the slow passion baffled her. He had only just touched her, and yet she already wanted to explode from the outside in. Her nervousness quickly dissipated when in one strong motion, he picked her up and placed her on the bed. His muscles bulged under the pressure of her body. Veins tore out to the front of his bronze skin. Yet, he didn't seem the least bit drained from her weight. He toted her as if she was a feather.

His intention was clear. He was not yet finished disrobing her. Going for the pants she clung to, he pulled them down slowly to see black panties that matched the discarded bra. Her large thighs were as perfect as her stomach and her shapely calf muscles astonished him. He looked at her manicured toenails and her soft feet and smiled.

"What?"she asked, uncomfortable again with him staring at her.

"You're so beautiful," he whispered, touching her waist.

She grabbed his hand. He wanted to take the last piece of clothing that made her safe. She looked into this eyes, begging his approval.

"LaToya, you're fascinating. Please, don't be shy," he assured in a soft, deep voice. His eyes twinkled. "I think that you're perfect."

She didn't believe him, but she did let go. Releasing his hand, she allowed him to pull her underwear away. His strong hands massaged her as he made his way down her legs.

For a moment, he paused with her panties still gripped in his hand as he pulled away. And in that moment, she wondered what he must think of her.

He trailed his hand back up her inner thigh brushing past the small strip of hair that hid her aching sex. Cream slicked her inner legs and soaked his fingers as he rubbed her. He slipped his finger in his mouth and tasted it. She closed her eyes for a moment, remembering what it felt like to be invaded. Her body clenched tight against his fingers as he returned them.

"You next," she taunted, opening her eyes.

He put his veined hand on his belt buckle and pulled away at the clasp all the while maintaining a naughty grin. His khaki pants were open now, showing black cotton underwear below. With a tug, he pulled them down past his elongated erection and shuffled them off along with his socks. Like a school boy, he stood in his glory breathing heavily and looking at his catch.

Only inches away from his penis, she felt her eyes lock in on him. What would he do now? She braced herself for anything. She wanted everything.

"Condom," he said more as a reminder to himself than to her. He walked away from the bed, revealing his perfect backside as he strode over to his dresser and pulled open the first drawer.

Digging under folded clothes, he pulled out a gold foil wrapper, tore the sheath with his teeth and looked down as his hands slid on the contraceptive.

LaToya watched curiously from bed. His chrome watch glimmered under the lamp as he prepared himself carefully. He looked back at her and smiled. Finished and ready, he turned around and walked back. His muscular, hairy legs were wide and perfect from years of playing soccer. She looked for any imperfections but could find none in his form.

"Can we turn off the light?" she asked, sitting up on her elbows.

"Why?" he stopped.

"I'd feel better," she soft softly.

Mitch walked back and turned off the light but walked to the window and opened the blinds to let the moonlight into the room. He wouldn't let her off that easy.

The darkness made LaToya feel a little better. It was intimidating to have such a good-looking, naked man about to make love to her, knowing that if she turned the wrong way, her ample tummy might spill over. At least, if he insisted on feeling it, he didn't have to see it.

She heard the bed creak a little as he crawled from the bottom. His eyes were focused, gleaming in the darkness as he arrived at the head of the bed. Instead of immediately invading her private space, he moved beside her and placed his elbow on the pillow. He stared in her eyes, giving her soul a moment to process the words that he would not say aloud.

"You're even more beautiful than I am," she said in a daze.

"Not in the least," he said, reaching over to stroke her long braids.

"Let it be good," she said in a whimpering voice. "Let it be better than anything that I've ever imagined. Please. I need it to be."

Mitch smiled. "Talk about pressure. Alright. I'll give you all that I have to offer. All I ask is the same from you."

"Agreed," she whispered against his hot skin.

LaToya felt him tug at her waist. Could it be that he wanted her on top? As heavy as she was, she found his request odd. Most men instantly went for missionary, but he seemed aroused by her thickness. He was flat on his back, muscles rippling through his stomach as he lifted his buttocks and bent his knees under her. Straddled on top of him, she leaned over and slowly kissed his lips. His hand slipped into her braids and pulled her face closer to his own. His other hand rubbed her ample bottom.

Taking a handful of her romp in his hand, he groaned and pulled her hair firmly in his hand.

"Ride me," he whispered in her ear. "I want to be deep inside of you right now."

She did as he said, intrigued by the fact that he could be a talker. Raising up, she felt his hand below guiding his thick, throbbing penis into her. Even wet, she was tight from years of abstinence. A painful pleasure erupted inside her as he lifted his buttocks and pushed, this time opening her body wide to his virile needs.

She didn't have a measuring stick but at that moment, she felt that she was stretched to the brim. It was almost too much. Gasping, she tried to adjust. But then a warm thumb brushed against her clit and caused her body to quake.

Throwing her head back, she forgot about her weight and slipped down his thick shaft into the ecstasy that awaited. A titillating wave of heat and wet sex rushed down her thighs in between them as they both rocked their hips into each other.

Mitch was gentle at first. Feet planted deep into the mattress, he carried them both into a rhythmic dance, rocking her body faster, driving deeper. His strokes were powerful thrusts of love and desire. She found the heady mix exhilarating. With his hands on her breasts, he moaned as she rode him, placing her own hands in his. Their fingers locked together. Her mouth parted and she said it. "Mitch," she whimpered. "I love you."

"Oh, LaToya, I love you," he answered in a growl. He pumped into her. "Do you like that?" he asked, looking up at her.

"Yes," she answered, skin humming. Spasms electrified her body.

"You feel so good," he said, pushing harder. "You look..." he groaned. "You look amazing."

LaToya then realized that he could see her in the moonlight. And he was looking at all her imperfections, all of her extra pounds. She tried to pull away, but he wouldn't allow it. Instead, he grabbed her by her full waist and pushed harder. Her body bucked against his thrusts, and she felt her knees shaking beside her.

He pulled her face to his again and kissed her passionately. His tongue slithered in and out of her mouth, softy then violently searching her mouth, coaxing her to give more of herself over to him.

Rolling them both over, he was behind her with one of his muscular legs cocked up as he pushed further. Another moan erupted from his throat. His hands held her in place, gripping her body and massaging her muscles. He enjoyed her anxiety. It aroused him to the point of sweat.

Biting his lip, he pushed into her again, enjoying the velvety feeling of her wetness. His hand was on her hip pulling her back as he braced himself. She cried out as she felt the first recognizable tremor. He moved her hair from her face and kissed her neck. His tongue slowly made evolutions around her sensitive ear before he bit it.

"Give it to me," he ordered as he whispered to her. "Stop worrying about everything and just submit to me."

"No," she said, enjoying him. "You have to make me," she said, allowing all of her inhibitions to give way to his taunts.

"Oh, now you feel like coming out to play," he smiled, biting her ear as he pumped inside of her faster. "

"Yes," she panted. "Yes. Yes."

"Well, come out." He pushed again. "Come," he taunted.

LaToya turned over with him now on top of her. She marveled at how different he was in bed. Normally, he was just a nice guy with a calm demeanor, but now he was foreboding and direct. He demanded her body with his carnal cravings.

Clenching his jaw, he moved over her and ran his hand down to her stomach. He looked at her and smiled. "Why did you keep this from me?" he asked, rubbing his knuckle over her throbbing clit again before he ducked to her mouth and kissed her parted, desperate lips. He bit the bottom lip, tugging at it as he pumped her harder.

Grabbing his penis, she ran it over her wetness and flicked its large head, sending a warm shudder through his groin. He groaned as she stroked him slowly, bringing him to a near climax.

He pulled away fast and slipped her nipple into his mouth. Again he returned to her perfect, succulent breasts. Sucking at her, he opened her legs as wide as they would go, feeling her body fight the unexpected.

"Neither one of us are going to orgasm for quite a while my dear, so you might as well stop the cheating, eh," he said with a grin before he moved his head down in between her thighs.

At that very moment, LaToya looked up at the ceiling fan, in the darkness of his room and forgot that she was a big girl, an ugly girl, a lonely girl. At that very moment, LaToya felt beautiful. Pulling at the sheets, clawing at the pillow, screaming his name, laughing at herself, fighting against his nimble tongue and curious fingers, she suddenly felt alive.

Chapter Eight

LaToya's eye resisted the sunlight as it flitted through the wooden blinds and shined in her face. Flapping her feet against the cover, she cupped her pillow, letting out a happy sigh and turned in the comfortable bed to realize that she wasn't at home. Mitch lay asleep beside her, resting comfortably with one arm around her and snoring lightly.

LaToya blinked hard. She had nearly forgotten what had happened last night, nearly forgotten that she had made love until the wee hours of the morning. Unashamed, she smiled and scooted closer to him, relishing in the body heat of another person. His virile scent was amazing. And it wall all over her, in her nose, on her lips, in her hair.

Prior to Mitch, she had been forced to endure an empty bed for far too long. She wanted to remember each sensation of what it was like, every smell, every sound, everything.

Mitch didn't stir. Instead, he slept even deeper with, if possible, pure contentment on his face. She looked up at him curiously. A small stubbly beard had appeared overnight.

Up close, she could see small wrinkles in his tanned face, and she noticed that he had somewhat large ears hidden behind his curly mass of hair. All perfect imperfections. Then the thought dawned on her. *What would he be like when he awoke and found her there?* He would see the small stretch marks that she had cleverly hidden the night before, the excess weight, the small scars from childhood. The big imperfections that were not perfect at all.

There was a familiar weight on her chest as she thought of the possibilities. It would be painful, if he woke and felt different from last night, but she braced herself for the possibility.

Placing her head on his chest, she listened to his heartbeat and enjoyed the moment. No matter what today brought, last night was amazing. They had been completely compatible in bed, turned on by the same things, attune to each other's needs. He had made good on his promise to fulfill her fantasies, taking her places that she'd never been with a man.

As she closed her eyes, she felt his fingers in her braids. She looked back up at him and watched the slits of his eyes open to deep green gems that sparkled at her in the morning light.

"Top of the morning to ya, lassie," he said in a guttural, low baritone.

"Hey yourself," she smiled.

Mitch frowned. "What?"

"What do you mean?" she asked, raising her head.

"You look like you want to say something, is all." He sat up a little. The bed creaked. She was surprised it wasn't broken after last night.

"I was wondering if you wanted to say something?" She waited on bated breath. "About last night."

Mitch face went blank for a minute and then a bright smile appeared on his lips. His furrowed brow straightened and his face lit up. His voice growled. "Last night was amazing. You were like a nimble little tomcat in bed. I would have never guessed, considering that you're so conservative all the time."

LaToya laughed.

"What else did you want me to say?" he asked, pulling her in to kiss her face. "Tell me, and I'll say it for you in seven languages."

"Nothing at all." She rubbed his chest. "Do you want some breakfast?"

"Sounds great," he looked in her eyes. "Wow. You're even prettier in the morning. You know that?"

"Thank you," she blushed. Pulling the covers around her, she tried to pull herself from the bed but felt his hand around her waist. She looked down at it, squeezing the cushiony extra skin, and she suddenly felt embarrassed.

"Do you think that maybe we could pick up where we left off last night before we go downstairs to breakfast?" he asked.

"More?" She bit her lip.

"It's just that," he pulled the covers from her body and looked at her naked form in the sunlight. "You look even better now that I can see you." He pulled her hand to his growing erection. "And I do love to watch."

LaToya melted down back into his warm embrace and felt him searching her mouth as he pulled her on top of him.

This is heaven, she thought blissfully.

***

By the time that LaToya got home, she had three messages on her phone. One from Mitch telling her that he already wanted her back. One from Deana to check on her after Sunday's fiasco. And one from Angela. Byron had evidently told Angela that he had fired her, but after last night, she really didn't care. Everything seemed to take on different meaning now.

It had taken everything in her to steal away from Mitch after breakfast, brunch and a late lunch. After sandwiches, wine and more mind-blowing sex, he had all but asked her to move in, which she had refused.

But still, even as she had driven away from him, she already missed him. She watched his muscular frame standing lonely in his driveway disappear in the rearview mirror and felt her chest constrict. She wanted to turn back and run back into his arms like some old love story. In fact, she had to think of reasons to leave. The pull to him was so strong until she needed a moment to clear her head. Falling in love was great. Falling so quickly and so hard was difficult to grasp. But he assured her that he felt the same – *assured her that he was in it for the long haul.*

As she went to her bathroom to run a bath, she glimpsed the weight scale in the corner. She gave it a conquering smile. He didn't care the least about her weight. And while she aimed to lose more for herself, for once, she didn't feel that it was a pre-requisite for a relationship.

The hot water clouded her thoughts as she eased into the bathtub. The warm water attached itself to the sore sensitive spots that Mitch had managed to leave on her.

Resting her head back, she closed her eyes and sighed deeply, finally feeling utterly exhausted. Nestling down in the comfort of her milk bath, she finally started to doze away when the phone rang.

She gazed over at the cordless phone and rolled her eyes. *Who could it be?*

Curious, she reached over and looked at the display. Angela. What did she want?

LaToya started to ignore it, but knew that Angela would just keep calling until she answered. With soapy arms and water dripping, she reached over and grabbed the receiver.

"Hello."

"LaToya," Angela said quickly. "I've been trying to call you for a day. Where have you been?"

LaToya was silent. She didn't owe her that explanation.

Angela immediately picked on it and smacked her lips. "I heard what Byron did. I'm trying to talk him back into..."

"Don't bother," LaToya interrupted. "I don't need his business that bad. I'll refer him to another service on Monday. I'm sure he'll be fine." She rested her head back down on the pillow in her tub and wiggled her toes.

"He's just really upset right now," Angela tried to explain. "This isn't easy for him."

"I'm sure it's not, but to be honest with you Angela, it's not my problem. He tried to make it be and that was his fault. I don't know who was most qualified for the job at their firm. But I do know that I was most qualified for mine. I did a good job for him, and just because I didn't jump on the band wagon with you, he fired me. So..." she rolled her eyes. "It's whatever, really."

Angela was taken aback. LaToya had always been level-headed and professional. She never got into name-calling or pissing matches with people, and normally, when she made her mind up, she stuck with it. However, she had always backed her – in her corner. Now, she was choosing this man, whom she claimed to have never slept with, over their friendship.

"Look, I don't want this to tear us apart. When Mitch is gone, we'll still need each other."

LaToya sat up in the tub. "What do you mean, when he's gone?" Her heart stopped. *Did the offer as partner mean that he would have to relocate? Oh, no.* She felt her breath catch in her chest.

"Well, when you all break up, because you know that men like that are just curious..." Angela sighed. "What I'm trying to say is that our friendship should outlast some man."

"Men?" LaToya shook her head. *This woman was impossible.* "If you had said when Mitch and Byron are gone, maybe I would be less offended. But it sounds like to me what you're implying is that I'm not good enough."

"LaToya, please don't tell me that you believe this man's lies." Angela flipped her keychain around her index finger and sat back in her office chair. "Of course, he's curious. You're something new. Something he hasn't experienced before, but when he gets familiar...."

"I've heard enough. You know, you've always thought that somehow, because you were lighter skinned, because you were smaller, because you dated more professional athletes, suddenly I was below you. Well, I'm not. It irks you to know that I have found a good man. It really irks you to know that I'm happy, and I don't need your approval. And it's killing your ass to know that my man is the one who was given this promotion. But Angela, honey, you're just going to have to deal with it."

With that LaToya ran her finger over the phone and turned it off. Smiling, she sat back in her tub and giggled.

***

The Hadley event was held at a massive mansion on the outskirts of town. The best and brightest of the firm along with other professionals from the city gathered under the cloudless night to commend the firm's annual accomplishments, pay homage to their clients and announce the newest partners.

When Mitch pulled up to the front of the mansion, the valet quickly ran out and opened the door for LaToya. Nervously, she got out and waited as Mitch made his way around the car to her. Taking her hand, he walked up the stairs to the front doors. He smiled proudly, holding her hand tightly and waving at the men who stood out front smoking cigars in their thousand dollar suits.

"I can feel your heartbeat through your hand, dear. Relax. You look beautiful," he said to LaToya as he opened the door for her.

"Easy for you to say. You look like a million bucks," she said, looking at him dressed up in a tuxedo that made him look like *James Bond.*

"Well, if I look like a million, you look like four million," he said, running his hand over her arm in her black gown that had been tailored to fit her body and expose her full cleavage. "Gosh, I hope that I can keep my mind off of those things long enough to get through the night," he said as he looked down at her breasts. "My mouth is already watering."

LaToya smiled. She had never met a man who loved her breasts as much as he did. At least once daily, he found a way to get them in his mouth and to get her in the bed.

As he opened the door for her, she walked in to find the house packed with socialites. In the main hall, a woman stood by the piano singing while the pianist played a slow tune. The house was lit up with sparkling lights and people in formalwear. Waiters and waitresses in black jackets and black pants served up expensive Hors d'oeuvres and flute glasses of expensive champagne.

"Thank you for doing this," Mitch whispered in her ear as he waved at another man. "I want to introduce you to some people."

As he escorted her across the large gathering, she caught a glimpse of Angela and Byron standing by the fireplace laughing and talking.

Angela's mouth dropped, and she stopped mid-sentence as she feasted her jealous eyes on her heavy-set friend. She had never seen LaToya look so beautiful. And she never thought in a million years that Mitch would have the audacity to bring her here among his peers and his bosses.

Within minutes, Mitch was introducing LaToya to the senior partners of the firm and their wives. He explained proudly that she was the owner of a thriving cleaning business and represented over ten employees who had impeccable backgrounds. The wives were impressed. They complimented LaToya on her dress, asked for her business card and shared with her their desire to find good staff for their homes.

Speechless, Angela watched in complete awe. Everything that she had said was falling apart. Her friend, the person whom she guessed would never even be acknowledged in these circles, was the center of attention. And they all accepted her, just as she was, because Mitch accepted her. And most importantly, because she accepted herself.

From the corner of her eye, LaToya saw Byron whisper something to Angela and point over in her direction, but Angela quickly nodded no and walked away.

LaToya smiled and held her head up high. As she went to the ladies' room, she passed a long mirror in the corner. She titled her head at her reflection. The beautiful, vibrant woman that she was looking at was her. It brought tears to her eyes, but she quickly pushed them away.

"I love your dress," a woman said as she passed. She stopped. "I'm Catherine. I understand that you're here with Mitch."

LaToya turned to the dark-skinned woman in a perfect black suit with red-backed heels, and a low fade and shook her head. "Yes, I'm his girlfriend," she said proudly. Just the mention of that fact made her smile.

"Well, it's very nice to meet you. I'm arriving late tonight. One of my kids was not feeling very well, but I wouldn't miss this event for the world. So, after I was sure that he was well *and off to bed*, I came on and left my husband to tend to him."

"How old is he?" LaToya asked.

"Ten years old now," the woman said, waving at a group of men who called out her name.

"Do you work with Mitch?" LaToya asked, clutching her purse.

"You could say that," she smiled. "I'm one of the founding partners. Catherine Severs."

"Of course," LaToya said, shaking her head. "Malone, *Severs*, Nelson and Crump." She extended her hand to shake the woman's hand. "Well, it's an honor to meet you."

"The pleasure is all mine, really. I've heard great things about you," Catherine said with a twinkle in her eye. "Now, if you'd excuse me. I really must go and say a few hellos, especially one in particular to the man of the hour, Mitch."

LaToya nodded and took a deep breath as the woman walked off. *Can't judge a book by its cover*, she thought to herself. Suddenly, she felt completely vindicated in her support of Mitch at Angela's house. In fact, she felt vindicated for everything. LaToya was sure that Angela didn't know that Severs was a dark, dark, black woman. That she had chosen Mitch over Byron. That the good ole boy network, while still working somewhere, wasn't necessarily working at this firm or in this case. And she only hoped that her old friend might find that out as well.

She quickly went to powder her nose and freshened up just in time to get back out to the main hall where the speech was to take place. As the crowd quieted, Catherine walked up to the front and was passed the microphone.

All eyes were on her. Smiles. Nods. Complete approval. She waved at LaToya in plain view of Angela, who looked on confused.

"We've had a great year here at Malone, Severs, Nelson and Crump, haven't we," Catherine said into the microphone.

The crowd cheered in response.

"You know when Mike, Bob, Cory and myself started this firm over twenty years ago, we had a vision for what we wanted to provide the world. And we've been able to see that vision come to fruition because of our clients and our staff. All of us have worked hard this year to accomplish our goals and take this firm to the next level. And I truly commend you all. But there is one man in particular who even in the face of adversity has done a tremendous job. He even took on a few projects that would have surely been halted if we had not had him step up and volunteer to take on his work and these extra assignments. Mitch O'Keefe, would you mind coming up here with me?"

The crowd cheered and clapped again, calling out his name. He slipped his hand from LaToya's and walked up to the front to join Catherine. Proudly, she placed her hand on Mitch's back and smiled.

"For many of you and because of the grapevine at the firm, I'm sure that you already know, but formally, I would like to announce our newest partner, Mitch O'Keefe, who has agreed to take us on long term and move our company into an amazing direction so that we can continue to flourish."

The crowd cheered him on and clapped. Gracefully, he nodded and waved towards the crowd, then threw a kiss towards LaToya.

Catherine continued. "I had the opportunity to meet his backbone, whom he has spoken so highly of at the firm for the last couple of weeks and she's amazing. I'm sure that both she and everyone here would like to hear a few words from you." She gave him a hug, then moved towards the background to give Mitch the stage.

Mitch smiled and slipped one hand in his pocket. He was a picture of elegance and confidence. His eyes glimmered. His bright, wide perfect smile exuded masculine beauty.

"You know, I'm really proud to accept this opportunity. And I'm honored to be here with you tonight celebrating our hard work as a cohesive team. It's been a trying but successful year for the firm, and I'm certain that as we move into the new fiscal year, we'll do even bigger and better things. When I accepted this partnership, Catherine asked me one question. She asked if I had someone at home to help keep me grounded." He turned and looked at Catherine. "And I answered *yes*. Everyone knows through the grapevine that I haven't been lucky in love, but let me tell you that the reason that I was able to pull myself up by the bootstraps and stay in the game..." He turned and looked at LaToya who stood with tears in her eyes and continued, "is because of my wonderful son, Zach, and the woman here with me tonight. She's been amazing and strong and a true vision for me. She's given me the strength to carry on, and she's given me the happiness I needed to feel whole again. So, I hope you all have the same or find the same, because I truly believe that happiness leads to better productivity at work, better outlooks on life and a stronger firm. So I'm happy to be a partner with this great organization, and I'm happy to have LaToya Jenkins as a part of my life."

The tears flowed freely down LaToya's cheeks. She didn't even bother to wipe them away. The entire crowd looked at her as they clapped. They cheered the two on as Mitch gave the microphone back and went down to hold her in his arms and kiss her for all to see. Even Angela wiped a tear. It was an eye-opener for anyone who had never seen it before. Love. Pure. Special. Genuine love. And it didn't matter that she was overweight. It didn't matter that she was dark skinned. It didn't matter that she was a cleaning lady. What did matter was that she was loved. And she loved. She gave her all and she received it back.

Holding him close, she whispered in his ear. "I don't feel like the ugly girlfriend anymore."

He looked into her eyes and smiled. "You were never *the ugly girlfriend* in the first place."

The End

Trivi's Charities of Choice

There are so many worthy charities that need your help. Please consider making a contribution to the following charities to help military men and women and their families in their time of need.

Semper Fi Fund
http://semperfifund.org/
Wounded Warrior Center • Bldg H49 •
Camp Pendleton, CA 92055
Phone: 760-207-0887
or 760-725-3680
Fax: 760-725-3685

Soldier's Angels
http://www.soldiersangels.org/
1792 E Washington Blvd
Pasadena, CA 91104

Wounded Warrior Project
http://www.woundedwarriorproject.org/
4899 Belfort Road, Suite 300
Jacksonville FL, 32256
Telephone: 877.832.6997
Fax: 904.296.7347

Whether time or money, consider giving back to the people who have already given so much.

STAY IN TOUCH

Official Author Website
www.latrivianelson.info

Email Latrivia Today
Latrivia@LatriviaNelson.com

Follow Latrivia on Twitter
www.twitter.com/Latrivia

Blog With Other Lonely Heart Fans
www.thelonelyheartseries.wordpress.com

"Like" The Lonely Heart Series
www.facebook.com/thelonelyheartseries

Become Friends on Facebook
www.facebook.com/latrivia.nelson

Visit Latrivia's YouTube Channel
www.youtube.com/Latrivia2009

The Grunt

Staff Sergeant Brett Black has a bad feeling that something is going to go terribly wrong. And as a Recon Marine, he pays attention to

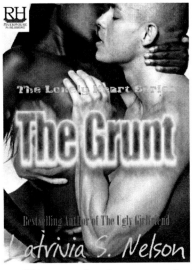

his gut. Only nothing can prepare him for what he encounters when he arrives at home from the base. His wife is leaving him, and there is nothing he can do about it.

Abandoned with a kid, the super alpha-male has to become domesticated quickly or find a willing substitute to help him with his son. Only the substitute he finds is no substitution.

Courtney Lawless is a true wild card. The budding librarian loves the classics and carries herself like a lady by day. But she also is full of life and surfs the waves of the Atlantic Ocean by night. Since her parents won't pay for college because of bad decisions in her past, the reformed bad-girl takes a job as Brett's live-in nanny to finish paying for school.

Brett has never seen a woman of such complex duality. Used to a wife who won't clean, cook or even talk to him, when he starts to live with Courtney, he realizes what he's been missing his entire life. Educated, amazing and refreshingly honest, the only thing that that this transparent beauty hides from her new boss is that she's also the Lieutenant Colonel's daughter.

Faced with another deployment to Afghanistan soon, the brooding Marine is forced to come out his shell to fight for what he loves, only this time, the war is at home.

Enjoy the interracial must-read romance of the summer, The Grunt, the third a longest book in Latrivia S. Nelson's Lonely Heart Series and today.

Third Book Book In Lonely Heart Series
ISBN: 978-0-9832186-4-7
Retail Price: $8.99

FINDING OPA!

What does the Greek word Opa mean? According to some it is a word or pronouncement of celebration; the celebration of life itself. It is another way of expressing joy and gratitude to God, life, and others, for bringing one into the state of ultimate wisdom.

Stacey Lane Bryant has three rules. She doesn't drive; she doesn't travel; and she most definitely will not date. From the outside, this odd-ball, thirties-something, single black woman is simply a creature of habit who has been beaten down by the tragedies of life. However those on the inside know that she's the widow of esteemed astro-physicist Drew Bryant, a highly sought after best-selling romance author and a devoted cat lover. The rules are simply designed to keep her safe and keep her sane.

However, some-one didn't tell the Greek bombshell, Dr. Hunter Fourakis, that rules weren't meant to be broken. While at his favorite pub, he eyes Stacey and instantly falls under her spell. Only, his rusty moves don't get him far with the brilliant introvert, who quickly leaves just to get out of his grasp.

What is meant to be will be, and the two run into each other in another chance encounter. This time Hunter is able to convince Stacey not only to go out on a spur-of-the-moment date with him but also to consider an unorthodox proposal that would benefit them both.

Hunter's late wife was killed while serving in Iraq, and he mourns every year for two months and three days. The mourning period is usually miserable for Hunter, but this time, he wants to celebrate life. Stacey's second romance novel is due to her agent in two months but is totally lacking motivation or passion, because she hasn't gotten over her late husband. Considering that they both need someone for a short period of time to fulfill very specific needs, they agree to be each other's help mate temporarily. Only as deprived widows, pressured professionals and lonely hearts, they find that while deadlines pass and mourning time ends, love lasts forever.

Read this romantic tale about two people who fight through tragic personal loss, family prejudices and age-old traditions to find good old fashion love in the second book of the Lonely Hearts Series, Finding Opa!

The Lonely Heart Series
Book Two
ISBN: 978-0-983-28647-9
$8.99

Dmitry's Closet

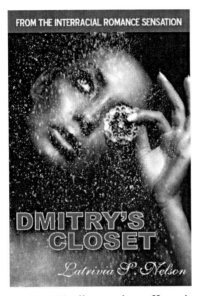

FROM THE INTERRACIAL ROMANCE SENSATION

From author Latrivia S. Nelson, author of the epic romance Ivy's Twisted Vine, comes a story about Memphis, TN, a deadly faction of the Russian mafia and an innocent woman who dismantles an empire.

Orphaned virgin Royal Stone is looking for employment in one of the country's toughest recessions. What she finds is the seven-foot, blonde millionaire Dmitry Medlov, who offers her a job as the manager of his new boutique, Dmitry's Closet. After she accepts his job offer, she soon accepts his gifts, his bed and his lifestyle. What she does not know is that her knight in shining armor is also the head of the Medlov Organized Crime Family, a faction of the elite Russian mafia organization, Vory v Zakone.

Falling in love with the clueless Royal makes Dmitry want to break his coveted code, leave his self-made empire and start a life far away from the perils of the Thieves-in-Law. Only, his brother, Ivan, comes to the Memphis from New York City bent on a murderous revenge.

With the FBI and Memphis Police Department working hard to build a case against Dmitry and his
brother trying to kill him, he is forced to tell Royal of
his true identity, but Royal also is keeping a secret -
one that changes everything.

Who will win? Who will lose? Who will die? Watch all
the skeletons as they tumble out of the urban
literature sensation Dmitry's Closet.

Warning: This book contains graphic language, sex,
and various forms of violence. However, it will also
melt your heart!

The Medlov Crime Family Series
Book One
Available in paperback and e-book format
ISBN: 978-1-6165874-5-1
Retail Price:$12.99

Dmitry's Royal Flush:
Rise of the Queen

From the popular multicultural author, Latrivia S. Nelson, comes the highly anticipated second install-ment of the Medlov Crime Family Series, Dmitry's Royal Flush: Rise of the Queen.

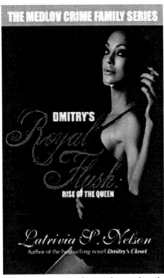

For Dmitry and Royal Medlov, money doesn't equal happiness. Forced to leave Memphis, TN and flee to Prague after a brutal mafia war, the couple nestled into the countryside to raise their daughter, Anya, and lead a safe, quiet life. But when Dmitry's son, Anatoly, shows up with an offer he can't refuse, Dmitry is forced to go back to the life he left as boss of the most feared criminal organization in world. Consequently, the deal could not only destroy the Medlov Crime Family but also Dmitry and Royal.

Royal hasn't been the same since she was attacked three years ago. Where she used to be a sweet, innocent girl, she's now the jaded, bitter mistress of the Medlov Chateau. However, a reality check is in store for the pre-Madonna when Anya's new teacher shows up with her sights set on stealing Dmitry, and

Ivan's old ally shows up with his sights on killing him. Can Royal save them all? Will she?

With a family in such turmoil, the only way to survive is to stick together. Read the gripping tale of a marriage strong enough to stand the test of time as Dmitry realizes that he has the best cards in the house as long as he has a Royal Flush.

The Medlov Crime Family Series
Book Two
Available in paperback and e-book format
ISBN: 978-0-5780601-1-8
Retail Price: $13.99

Anatoly Medlov: Complete Reign

From the bestselling series, the Medlov Crime Family, comes the highly-anticipated story about America's favorite bad boy...

Anatoly Medlov is the youngest crime boss in the Medlov Organized Crime Family's history. Now, he has to prove himself to a council who thinks his legacy has not been well-earned, amidst a grueling investigation by Lt. Nicola Agosto of the Memphis Police Department and during plot to destroy him by his ex-lover, Victoria. In his loneliness, the only one he can confide in is the shop girl, Renee, an old friend who knows more than anyone about his personal journey. However, his friendship soon turns to love for a woman he knows that he cannot have because of the feared code his is bound to by the Vory v Zakone.

When his estranged mother dies suddenly, Anatoly flies to Russia to pay his last respects and discovers a jolting secret. The late Ivan Medlov's own brutal legacy still lives through his son, Gabriel, and his New York crime family. Anatoly's father and former Czar of the underworld, Dmitry, sees this as an opportunity to unite the two major families and blesses both men. However, Anatoly sees Gabriel as a threat to his empire and competition for the affection of his father. Will cousins kill because of the sins of their fathers?

Gabriel Medlov has always resented his existence. Now as an undercover DEA agent, he plans destroy the Medlov Crime Family once and for all. Only in order to get close enough to destroy the organization, he must also get close enough to love his estranged family. Will blood prove thicker than water or will one man's revenge end the Family for good?

Follow the story of one young man who fights to be king in a room full of royalty and suffers the pain of his position in the romantic suspense guaranteed to make you want more.

The Medlov Crime Family Series
Book Three
Available in paperback and e-book format
ISBN: 978-0-9832186-1-6
Retail Price: $14.99

Upcoming Books

The Lonely Heart Series:
Gracie's Dirty Little Secret
Taming the Rock Star
Unleashing the Dawg
The Pitcher's Last Curve Ball
The Tragic Bigamist
The Credit Repairman

The Medlov Series:
Saving Anya

The Chronicles of Young Dmitry Medlov:
Volume 4-8

The Agosto Series:
The World In Reverse

The Married But Lonely Series:
Forgive Me
Sexting After Dark

Paranormal Books
Funny Fixations
The Guitarist
The Pain of Dawn

The Nine Lives of Kat Steele:
Volumes 1-9

***Books will be released during 2011 & 2012, but dates are
tentative so please visit website for updates.***

About the Author

In the last three years, bestselling author Latrivia S. Nelson has published ten novels including the largest interracial romance novel in the genre to date, *Ivy's Twisted Vine* (2010), The Medlov Crime Family Series and The Lonely Heart Series. She is also the President and CEO of RiverHouse Publishing, LLC, the wife of retired United States Marine Adam Nelson, the mother of two beautiful, rambunctious children and working diligently on her Ph.D.

When she's not busy writing novels, doing homework or running a publishing company, Nelson spends her time at princess tea parties with her daughter, Tierra, or being saved by her super hero son, Jordan, during playtime, cooking great meals for the family and watching the sunset with her best friend and real-life super hero, Adam.

Attention Future Romance Authors:

Do you have a romance novel or short story that you want to share with the world? Is it edgy? Is it romantic? Is it erotic? Is it unpublished?

Latrivia S. Nelson and RiverHouse Publishing are going to launch a **e-book only imprint** in the Summer of 2012, Love Only.

We will begin accepting submission in January 2012 and will announce the authors in April of 2012. For more information, please contact Latrivia S. Nelson via email at Lnelson@RiverHousePublishingLLC.com.

The Home of Bold Authors with Bold Statements.
www.riverhousepublishingllc.com